A Woman in New York

A tale of three lives

By Lou Spaventa

Love is wise; hatred is foolish.
Bertrand Russell

*Thanks for
your help, Karl.*

Lou

Acknowledgements

I would like to acknowledge, first and foremost, the help and support of my wife, Marilynn, whose keen eye kept my errors to a minimum, and whose woman's perspective kept me from overloading testosteronic prose in this novel. I would like to acknowledge Bill Spencer, whose technical facility, calm demeanor and artistic eye have made this novel a reality for me. Finally, I say thank you to Frank Lazorchik for being a patient reader and for correcting my failing Italian.

■ Lou Spaventa ■

Table of Contents

Table of Contents
(continued)

CHAPTER ONE:
Johnny

The sweat began to pour off my neck into my collar and dribble down my chest as soon as I got off at Marcy Avenue, heading towards the Marcy Houses. I walked down to Ellery Street into public housing and up a flight of stairs. The stench of urine and cheap wine filled the stairwell. I had a client in this stew of failed humanity. She was a white woman in a black and tan neighborhood, out of place just like me, but at least I got paid for it. Ella had been turning tricks since she was sixteen when she ran away with her meth head boyfriend to the streets of New York from her suburban teen life on the Island. The boyfriend got cut up bad in a drug deal gone south. He went back to Great Neck and left Ella on the street. She had no skills, but a tight little body. She began to sell it, and the more she sold it, the cheaper she got. She wound up the workhorse whore of a mean Puerto Rican pimp named Jimmy D. He set her up in a one bedroom dump, kept her high and needy, and ran her ten hours a day. By the age of eighteen, Ella looked thirty. She was nearly twenty now, according to her records with New York City Social Services. She looked forty. Her blond hair was thinning. Her breasts were sagging. Her skin was blotched and her eyes were sunken deep into their sockets. She barely spoke anymore, save when she was hustling on the streets. At first Jimmy D ran her in midtown Manhattan. When she got skaggy, he brought her into lower rent Chinatown, and finally to Brooklyn. And when she began to look so bad that no one would pay for her, he beat her, taking out his anger at the white world on his white whore. She was my client and therefore my responsibility. She had no visible means of support except for a part time gig at a local laundromat that paid her minimum wage for ten hours of work a week, not enough for food, for rent, for the cigarettes she smoked one after the other. I was charged with getting her life back on track, a task I felt was pointless. I pegged her for human flotsam, soon to go down the East River to oblivion. In the meantime, I was supposed to help her, so I rapped hard three times on her door. This was our signal. Ordinarily, she didn't answer the door because only problems came through the threshold. Ella opened the door to me.

"Hey, Ell, howya doin'?"

"I'm bad, Johnny. I can't even stand up I'm so weak."

"What happened?"

"Jimmy beat me bad 'cause I can't work no more."

"Ella, that work is the kind of work that got you where you are. That and your meth addiction."

"Yeah, I know."

"Have you tried to contact your father?" Ella's father disowned her when she ran away with Bobby Jeter, her mulatto boyfriend from the underclass of

Great Neck. No daughter of his was going to fall in with a lower class colored boy. But, of course, he never said that although everything he did implied just that. Ella's mother had died giving birth to her and this was the first wrong that her father felt Ella had done him. He remarried when she was ten, and her stepmother wanted little to do with her. So Ella lived, isolated in her own home, with neither a father nor mother who would love and care for her. I had to ask her a stupid question like I did because it was part of my visit protocol. I knew that Ella's father didn't care about her and wouldn't lift a finger to rescue her from her miserable life of buying meth and selling her body. Somewhere inside me I felt for her, so I often lingered at her apartment and talked to her as if she were just fine. I knew she liked that, the feeling that someone treated her as if she wasn't human trash. Once I stayed too long. I met Jimmy D. He burst in, looked at me, then looked at Ella and said, "He best be payin' bitch or you're gonna be black and blue on that white skin of yours." I introduced myself to Jimmy then, explained to him who I was and why I was there. Once he knew that, he had no use for me.

4

With a stiletto in his right hand that he flicked open and then closed in a sick rhythm, he said, "Whyncha fuck off Mr. City Social Worker? You cuttin' in on her work time." I saw the menace in Jimmy's eyes and felt that he wouldn't mind cutting me if I challenged him.

"I'll be off then, Miss Winters. I'll see you next month. Please check in if you need anything in the meantime."

"Yeah, she need to work, motha fucka. Get out."

So I did.

For the New York City Department of Social Services, Ella was an outlier. She didn't fit in any of the common categories for women except for domestic violence, but she wasn't in a legal relationship with Jimmy D and she would never claim on paper that Jimmy D was abusing her. Once I tried to get her help without her knowing, and it only made things worse. She got a severe beating for "tryin' ta leave me bitch," according to Jimmy. I met her at the Family Health Center on Fulton Street the day after he beat her. Her face was swollen so badly that her facial features were hard to discern. She was hunched over because Jimmy had repeatedly punched her in the stomach and kicked her in the vagina. I will never forget the look of agony and fear on her face. The admitting doctor knew what had happened, but Ella claimed she had fallen down a flight of stairs. She refused to accuse her tormentor. She only began to be open about it to me when, in return for allowing me to visit her, I promised not to take legal action against Jimmy again without her permission.

These dreams, I should say this dream, it keeps reoccurring in slightly different ways, but it's always me in trouble and a red headed woman saving me. I know she's beautiful, but I can't make out her face. I am drowning in a backyard pool in the Hamptons. She is sitting in a lounge chair with her top down, tanning herself. I start swallowing water. For some reason, I can't swim, but I really can. It's like when you have those times between dream and waking when you see bad things happening but you can't move to avoid them. The red head looks at me swallowing water. I say nothing, just allow myself to sink down into the sun bright pool water. Then she dives in and pulls me by the arm to the shallow end of the pool. Before I can thank her, I wake up.

Ella Winters is in awful shape in every way. She is physically, mentally and spiritually empty and hurting. I don't think she is going to last out the year, maybe even the summer. It's been so hot these past weeks that I wish I was out on the Island, somewhere, maybe Ronkonkoma, swimming in the depths of that lake. Anywhere but here in this shabby, steaming hot public housing one bedroom with this sad, sick junky girl.

"Ella, have you been to the rehab clinic?"

"Can't, Johnny. Jimmy D won't let me."

"Why not then?"

"Says I'm his bitch and I do what he says, no reason needed."

"You gotta get away from him, Ell."

"I know, Johnny, but I ain't got a place to go to."
She says this looking at me as if I will supply that

place for her. "You can help me Johnny. I'd be good to you," she says, spread eagle on a filthy white couch.

"That's not what I want, Ella."

"What do you want, Johnny?"

"I just wanna do my job. Help you get on your feet." I say this, but she doesn't believe it and I don't either. I go through my litany of questions and she gives me the answers she knows I need. Then I leave.

"Next time, Ella."

"Yeah, Johnny. Next time."

It's two o'clock in the morning and quiet in Bay Ridge. No traffic noise. No honking horns or highway buzzing. I like where I live. It's where I grew up. Instead of my grandma's semi-detached red brick house off Seventh Avenue, I'm down by the water. I can see the Narrows from my apartment window. Even on the hottest summer day, I get a breeze off the water. Water makes me happy. It speaks of release, ease, lightness of being. I'm a swimmer, not a common thing for a Brooklyn boy, but just what the doctor ordered when I was young and suffering asthma attacks. My lungs got strong from hours in the Y pool. I swam in college, for a small Catholic school in North Carolina. As soon as I graduated I came back home. I'll never leave Brooklyn. Bet on it.

It's two o'clock, and someone is tapping, scratching at my apartment door. Who the hell could it be? No friends or family would do such a thing. I sit up in bed and listen. It continues. I get up, go to the bathroom to fetch my robe, and I approach the door. The scratching and tapping continue.

"Yeah?"

"Johnny? Johnny, it's me."

"Me who?"

"Me, Ella."

"You know what time it is?"

"I'm sorry, Johnny, but you gotta help me. I ran

away from Jimmy D."

"Oh, fuck! Does he know where I live?"

"No, Johnny. Johnny open the door, please. Please Johnny."

I do and she stumbles in. She's a mess. Her sheer white blouse is torn from the neck to the waist. Her face is red with blood tricking down from her head. I can see the wound on her scalp. She has on two mismatched sandals, and a pair of black shorts. No underwear.

"Geez, Look at you!"

"He was gonna kill me, Johnny. I had to leave."

"How'd you know where I live?"

"One visit to the Marcy you used the bathroom at my place, so I took the chance to look into your wallet. You left it in your coat jacket. I read your address and memorized it just in case."

"Just in fuckin' case? God, girl! What am I gonna do with you?"

Ella starts crying, and I give in.

"Okay, I'm gonna run the water in the shower. You get in and scrub yourself clean. Christ you stink of beer and sweat."

"He brought his posse to the apartment. They were drinking and they did me, three of them."

"Too much information, Ella."

She comes out of the shower and I wrap a large bath towel around her. Her body is so thin, it makes me sad.

"Ella, I gotta blow-up single, but it's kinda late to inflate it now. So, you can sleep in my bed and I'll take the couch. Best that way. You don't know your way 'round my place and I do. Oh yeah, and I'll get you something to put on. Probably one of my tee shirts would work for you."

She followed my directions without a word. I heard my summer quilt swish over her body and saw the night table lamp go dark. So, I closed my eyes and then the dream came.

It was the red head again. This time I could make out a bit of her face; she had high cheekbones I thought, but I couldn't make out her eyes, her nose, her lips. Weird, how it was just the cheekbones! Now I'm in a room, and there's water seeping in, not real quick, but very steady. As the minutes pass and the room fills, I realize that I can't get out and that I'm gonna drown. I know the red head is on the other side of the door, but I can't tell her I'm in trouble. I don't know why, but I can't talk. The water is now up to my chin and I'm treading water; it's not easy to do. I'm getting tired. I have just enough room to gulp breaths, then the water covers me. I'm done for. The door opens. The water floods away. I'm standing on the floor. There she is, opposite me, smiling, but I can't see her face. How do I know she's smiling? She turns her back and walks away. I start to follow her. Then I wake up.

I spent a weekend in the apartment with Ella. She was going cold turkey, but God she was driving me nuts. She couldn't sit still. "I'm cold, Johnny."

"Here, put on my flannel shirt, but God. The tee shirt is covered with blood. You can't wear it. Take it off."

"Sure, Johnny." And she took it off right in front of me. She had no shame. I wondered how that happened to a woman. She looked at me as I averted my eyes from her bare breasts. A half hour later, "Johnny, I'm so hot. Let's go for a walk outside."

"What are you gonna wear?"

I had washed her shorts, but she had no underwear and only two mismatched sandals for footwear. We went to the Avenue to a cheap clothing store. I spent a hundred on her for clothes. Lucky for me it was summer, and girls didn't need so much or it would've been a lot more.

She swore she'd pay me back, but I just wrote it off as good money gone. Would be worth it if I could get her out of the apartment.

She wouldn't eat, but I forced her to drink a protein shake I made with whey powder, berries, yogurt and a banana. I had all I could do to keep up with her junkie skittishness. One good thing happened that weekend. I convinced her to get into a residential program the city was running in Bay Ridge.

It was in a group home near Cannonball Park down by the bridge. She was almost twenty years old and could make her own legal decisions. Thank God she signed herself in on Monday morning.

"You'll call me tonight, Johnny, right? You won't leave me by myself. I don't know no one here."

"Yeah, I'll call, Ella. Just make sure you focus on getting clean. You and I know it ain't gonna be easy."

"How do you know, Johnny? You never been a junkie."

"Yeah, but I lived with one growing up. My cousin Gino lived with us: he was on heroin from his freshman year in high school. Threw away an athletic scholarship because of the horse. You know I don't even know where he is today. When I left for college, that was the last I saw him."

"Sorry, Johnny."

"Nah, water under the bridge, kid. Just get

clean."

I felt good that week. I called her every night, and she sounded like she was doing well. She said she wasn't using, not even tempted she said. I should've known good things wouldn't last 'cause that Friday as I flopped down on the sofa with a can of Bud in my hand and the Mets on the tube, there was a knock on my door. Nobody I know or care about ever knocks. We text. We call. Whatever. I opened to a wild-eyed Jimmy D.

Coño, where's the little *puta, ese?*"

"Jimmy, she ain't here."

"Bullshit, Mr. Social Work. She came here last week. Doncha think I know that? Stupid little *puta* thinks I can't figure her out. She lef' your name an' address onna wall near the phone. 'Johnny it says. 212 Ridge Boulevard, Apartment 3C.' So where the fuck is she, *coño?*"

"Got me, Jimmy D."

"Lissen, you tell me or I'll cut you up bad, *ese.*"

Jimmy stepped toward me into the apartment, and I immediately twisted his left arm behind his back, kicked him in the back of the knee and pushed him face down on the floor. "Been wantin' to do this for a long time, but, you know, I'm a social worker, weak and all on the job. But you're trespassin' Jimmy, so I got every right to take you down. Now listen to me. You're gonna get up and turn around and walk out of this apartment and as soon as you do, you're gonna forget I live here. Got it?" And with that I twisted his left arm a bit further towards the back of his head until he screamed an agreement. I also fleeced him while I had him down and removed the blade from his front pocket. "I'll take this as a souvenir, *coño?* Okay with you?"

I helped Jimmy up, turned him around, and kicked him as hard as I could in the ass, propelling him down the first flight of stairs. "That's for treating her like an animal, you bastard. I never wanna see your face again."

I had a hard time falling asleep that night, wondering whether I had really had an effect on

16

Jimmy D. He was a hard scrabble kid from the streets. I know he had to fight for everything he had. I hoped that he didn't value Ella enough to keep coming after her or me. I woke up at three o'clock from a dream about the redhead.

She was smiling at me as I was drowning in the waves at Manhattan Beach. It was a September hurricane and the waves were over eight feet high. The surf was treacherous. I was the only one in the water. I reached for her hand. I needed help. That's when I awoke and stared at the far wall for what seemed like an hour, but when I picked up my phone, it said 3:05. I tossed and turned until day broke over the Narrows. I put on my sweats and shoes and ran the walkway by the water for a few miles. I stopped for a grande cappuccino at a Starbucks on the way back. The barrista had a big toothy smile and the most intense red hair I'd ever seen. I don't know how anyone could be that friendly at six in the morning, but she was. I thought to myself, "A big jolly Irish lass, freckles all over her body I'll bet." When I got back to the apartment, my voice mail showed five missed calls. I didn't care. I showered and went back to bed. I'd earned a decent few hours sleep.

CHAPTER TWO:
Two: Ella

When I look at myself in the mirror, I feel sad, sad that I let these years go by without taking charge of my life, sad that I let men use me for their own reasons. Things are different now. Johnny doesn't know it, and I think he doubted I would last a week here in rehab, but I'm getting stronger.

Although Johnny calls me often, I really don't think I need his phone calls for support. There's a motto here: "You are your own best support system." And I am. I have a routine now, a rhythm to my days, and it's one that I created for myself. I am using this rehab center to build myself into the woman I want to be. I will change a lot, and that scares me. But I know that it's something I need to do. I'll start with my language, drop the junkie talk, speak like I was educated to speak.

They tell me I have freedom here, but it's not freedom I crave. I thought when I ran away with Bobby Jeter that we were going to be free, free of my cold bastard of a father and bitch of a stepmother. And how did that turn out? With him running back home and leaving me on the streets at sixteen. I realize now it's not freedom, it's purpose. That's what makes a life. It's the routine I've created for myself, the discipline I've imposed on myself that is going to help me find my purpose.

I look in the mirror. I look hard and I get beyond the sadness of time wasted, beyond the feeling of emptiness I carried these past years inside me. Now I notice I can breathe. I can see clearly. The meth head that was me is gone. I am sure of it. As sure as I've been of anything. And I'm getting healthy. For the past few years, I had no idea what that meant. Now I see my skin is beginning to regain its color. The pallor is gone. My skin turns red when I rub it. It doesn't bruise at the slightest touch as it did when I was on meth. I don't have red blotches all over and my skin doesn't feel as if bugs are crawling all over it. I've stopped picking at my face. Thank God, I haven't lost any teeth to meth! Another year on it and I would probably be a candidate for an oral surgeon.

Now I'm getting better, stronger and finding myself as a woman. The mirror doesn't lie. I still have a long way to go. It's only been a month in rehab, but I'm starting to feel the power I have inside me. I notice some of the guys in the program looking me over now. The first day I was here, everyone looked away. They'd all seen meth heads and they knew I was one.

The others here, well some are meth heads, others are on heroin, coke or prescription drugs. But I gotta say that the meth heads who came into the program looked the worst of all when they got here, and I was one of them.

What I like about the program is the emphasis on

the individual person, none of this gotta-be-in-a-group, like some sort of cut rate confessional with the therapist as priestess. Me, I have a routine. I go to yoga class first thing. That's at six o'clock. Then I have a glass of juice and a piece of fruit. I walk out of the rehab home onto the street and start my jog along the water. I drink in the sea breeze, foul or fair. Back at the rehab home, I eat a bowl of yogurt, fruit, and black coffee. Then I start work on my GED. I never finished high school, but I'm no dummy. I know I need education to get ahead. Lunch is a big salad with fresh greens and vegetables. After lunch, I take advantage of the afternoon programs. I'm pretty good with numbers and with computers. I took the first level bookkeeping course and continued on my own, doing self-study with the computer as teacher. At night, I read. Just about anything. We get the Times and I check the bestseller list on Sundays. I pick out one fiction and one non-fiction book a week. I go to the local library and check them out. If they're already gone, I ask the librarian for another book by the same writer or another book on the same subject. I've gotten to know the librarian, Willy Jefferson, a sharp, strong black woman. She's my role model right now. I want to be as good at my job as Willy is at hers. I want to be as sure of myself as she is. She started our relationship by asking me about myself one Monday morning.

"Hey, missy, I've been wondering about you. You look like you're getting over some kind of illness, something bad. You wanna talk about it?"

"You're right. About four years of being a methamphetamine addict. I live in the rehab home just near Cannonball Park. But why the interest?"

"Why? Cause I haven't seen a woman your age, black, white, brown, green or yellow, take out books each week and return them the next as if you've read them."

"I have."

"And why the interest? Most young women your age are focused on their smart phones."

"Truth is I don't have anyone to share with right now, and I could care less about it. I'm working on myself."

"And part of that work is self-education?"

"Yes. Who else is responsible for my education if it's not me?"

"Your parents?"

"Mother's long dead. Father might as well be."

"I get it. Well, these days being a librarian is a pretty lonely job until the grade school kids pour in, and then the conversation is not at the highest level, so…feel free to stop in and chat."

"Thanks, I'd like that. The sign says your name is Wilhelmina Jefferson."

"Call me Willy."

"Thanks, Willy. I'm Ella."

"See you then, Ella."

"See you, Willy."

And that began my first internship in becoming a

woman. Wilhelmina Jefferson taught me that opportunity is everywhere if you just keep your eyes open and know what it is you're looking for. In my case, I was looking for a mentor, someone I could learn to imitate. Willy was that person for me. She came from the Bronx, from the worst of the housing projects. I knew something about that environment from the Brooklyn side thanks to Jimmy D. But unlike me, Willy had a loving mother who worked three part-time jobs to take care of herself, and her five children. Of those five children, Willy was the only one to escape the ghetto. The other four were life's lottery losers. The boys were inside, and the girls dropped out of school, got pregnant and went on welfare. Whatever it was that made Willy different, she never said, and I don't think she knew, but she had the drive to succeed. Graduated near the top of her class in high school, went to Queen's College, moved out on her own, worked a fulltime job, and finally got a degree in library science. Willy had an apartment on Shore Road. I soon got used to spending time with her on the weekends.

I've let Johnny know that once a week is just fine for phone calls. It's mid-October and I have six weeks left here in the group home. I feel so good, better than I've ever felt about myself. I love to run in the cool fall weather, to kick my feet into the swirling russet leaves the wind blows around Shore Road Park. I look out into the Narrows and track the white caps as they collide with the freighters going north and south. I look up into the blue sky at noon. It's glorious! I'm glorious! I'm a whole person. My body is strong and getting stronger. My mind is focused. I am beginning to figure out my path. I can almost see it in my mind's eye.

I look at the Verrazano Bridge, and I see what humans can do with their lives. Somebody designed that bridge. Somebody built it. It has a purpose and it serves thousands of people. I looked up Giovanni da Verrazano, the Italian explorer who sailed for Spain looking for a route to the Pacific Ocean. He "discovered" New York harbor and the bridge bears his name. That was nearly five hundred years ago. I try to imagine what he would think if he sailed into that harbor now. Too bad for him, the natives in the Caribbean made him their dinner on his final voyage to the Americas. I guess that's, whatcha call it, a metaphor for life: some eat and some get eaten. Up to now, I was in the last category, but no more. I think about the last session I had with Merry Elliot, the shrink who does these one-on-ones with us.

"So, things have been going well for you, Ella? Getting better?"

Before I speak, my eyes focus on "The Gestalt Prayer" that hangs in a picture frame on Merry's office wall.

I do my thing and you do your thing.

I am not in this world to live up to your expectations, and you are not in this world to live up to mine.

You are you, and I am I,

and if by chance we find each other, it's beautiful.

If not, it can't be helped.

(Fritz Perls, *Gestalt Therapy Verbatim*, 1969)

"Is that what you think, Merry? That people find each other or not? That if they do it's beautiful, and if not it can't be helped? How can you be a therapist if you're okay with giving up on some of your patients?"

"We are who we are right here and now, Ella, not any time before or after. We can only connect now. But tell me, what are you feeling inside? How are you, Ella?"

"I'm fine I told you, better than I've ever been. But tell me, Merry, how is it that you work to make people feel better if the responsibility is theirs alone? Isn't there some sort of contradiction there?"

"This has nothing to do with anyone else but you and me at this moment. Are we connecting? I am here doing my work with you. If it helps you, that is good."

"It just doesn't make sense to me, but I am better and you are part of that, so thanks, Merry."

"Thanks are not necessary. I have done my work well with you and that's what counts, what ultimately makes me satisfied with myself."

"So it's all about the self: myself, yourself?"

"I believe that's the way it is."

"I see."

Yes, I see. I see what a successful woman focuses on. She focuses on work. Willy and Merry are from different worlds; Merry grew up on the upper East Side in a ten room "apartment." Both women put their energy into their work, and achieve success through it. Not babies, not husbands, not possessions, but achievement through work that they chose. Being good at doing something is feeling good about yourself. That is my missing piece. I need to find out what it is that I can do. Next week is Thanksgiving week, the first week of the shopping frenzy. It's when I get out of here for a weekend. Johnny's invited me to have Thanksgiving dinner with him and his family. He says he has a job lead for me if I'm interested. I am. What is it? Will I like it? I wonder whether it might be a first step to a career. I need to think. A lot is going to happen in the coming days, and I want to make the right choices.

CHAPTER THREE:
Thanksgiving Italian Style

I am spending Thanksgiving with Johnny and his extended family down on President Street, where his family occupies an entire brownstone. The neighborhood was changing, but there were old Italian families, some of them with ties to the Mafia, that hung on. Johnny picked me up in his Prius and we were there inside of twenty minutes from Bay Ridge, taking the BQE. We parked in front of his mother's brownstone, but not before a man the size of a large refrigerator came into view in the front windshield.

"Dachew, Giovanni? Johnny Do-Good?"

"Yeah, Rocco. It's me."

"Who's the broad? She ain't lookin' like a *paisana*."

"Her name's Ella Winters. Ella say hello to Rocco Lo Presti."

"Pleezameecha, Honey."

"Same here, Rocco."

Rocco turned to Johnny again. "Good to see you Johnny Do-Good. Ya still doin' good, no?"

"Yeah, Rocco. Still tryin'."

"Good for you, den."

And with that, Rocco returned to a chair that he had been occupying on the stoop of the brownstone next to Johnny's mother's.

"What was that about, Johnny?"

"You've heard that this area had a few families connected to the Cosa Nostra? Well Rocco is a soldier, *un soldato*, in one of them. That's why he's out there keeping an eye on the neighborhood. It didn't use to be that way. No one ever came here who wasn't part of the neighborhood or connected, "

"And now?" I asked Johnny,

"Now it's the Russians, the Bloods, the Crips, MS13, the Sureños. The Mafia is hard pressed to hold its own in the crime world these days. Anyway, let's go in and meet the clan. Be prepared. There'll be a lot of people, all giving you the once over, trying to figure out what you're doing with me or what I'm doing with you."

So, we went in and I met Johnny's mother, a woman in her late fifties who dressed in a black silk dress and cardigan. From leafing through fashion mags at the rehab home, I guessed her clothes were from Saks Fifth Avenue. An Italian widow in black looked a little different these days. Mrs. Rosso had a trim figure, lively blue eyes, and blond hair going gray. She was a handsome woman, and I could tell by looking at the way she held herself that she was used to being in command of every situation she was in.

This was her home. She was in charge. She looked me in the eye when we were introduced.

"Isabella Rosso. Pleased to meet you."

"Hello, Mrs. Rosso. I'm Ella Winters, a former client and now a friend of your son."

"Johnny's told me about you, but he neglected to say how lovely you are." She gripped my hand in a strong, nearly masculine handshake.

"Three months ago you wouldn't have said that. I owe your son a lot. He helped me get back on my feet."

"So, I've heard. Johnny's always been a good boy; takes after his uncle Vito, a Dominican priest. They both have that save-the-world mentality. It's rare in a Sicilian, you know. We've had a long history of trying to save ourselves from the world." And she smiled, releasing my hand.

So, began a long day of eating and greeting. Johnny had more brothers, aunts, uncles, cousins, and assorted distant relations than I thought could ever fit at one table. But there they all were, eating lasagna and turkey, an Italian-American Thanksgiving. The men were dressed in dark suits with bespoke shirts and beautiful silk ties. By the time the fruit and cheese came around, the whole of them had their jackets off and their ties loosened. But the women, elegant each one, remained as they were: beautifully dressed, perfectly coiffed, every hair in place. Before the guests divided into men playing pinochle and women preparing pastries and coffee, Johnny asked me to take a walk around the block with him. The early evening air was bracingly cold after the cauldron of Mrs. Rosso's home.

The sky was growing dark as we walked down the steps of the brownstone. "So what did you think, Ella?"

"You've got a very strong woman for a mother, and you've got more relatives than there were people in my neighborhood in Great Neck. And it's cold." At that, Johnny moved to draw me close to him and I let him. I felt there was a debt that had to be repaid in some way. Of a sudden, something caught my eye and it made me shiver.

"Johnny, I saw someone, someone I never thought I'd see again. It was Jimmy D. I think I just saw Jimmy D."

"That's impossible. It'd be suicide for a PR gang banger to show his face around here."

"Yeah, you're probably right, Johnny." I looked again, but there was no one.

Jimmy D was watching from behind a hedge row across the street from the Rosso's brownstone.

That's right, bitch, you saw me. I been watchin' you two since you got here. I'm gettin' me some back today. It's my Thanksgiving. By the end of the night, you'll be thanking me for helping you escape that bunch of hasbeen Guineas. You'll see who I am now. No one pushes Jimmy D around. No Guinea social worker. No one runs away from me. Not you Ella Winters. I've gotcha both. You'll be payin' me back tonight.

When I walked Ella back to the house, I saw Rocco on the stoop. I thought to go in and bring a *canolo* and a *demitasse* out to him. He was still sitting in the chair on the stoop of the Gaetas' home next door. I approached him. He seemed very still, which was strange because he had this nervous habit of putting his right hand in his pocket and jiggling his change around.

"Rocco? Hey, Rocco! Look what I brought."

The hole in his forehead was so small and neat that, at first, I didn't see it. I dropped the pastry and the coffee and ran inside.

"Mamma, Someone shot Rocco!"

Mamma turned to her two oldest.

"Gennaro, Gildo, go see what happened. Johnny, you stay here with the girl."

It was two o'clock in the morning before my mother would let me drive Ella back to Bay Ridge. As

37

we got in the car, and I warmed up the engine, both of us looked around for any sign of a threat. The Rosso and Gaeta men had been all over the neighborhood for the last five hours. I couldn't imagine there'd be anyone foolish enough to stay around after what happened. But I was wrong. Just before we got on the BQE, a black Navigator cut me off and stopped right in front of my Prius. Then two more came on either side of me.

Jimmy D got out of the first Navigator.

"Open the door, Guinea boy. Open up or I'll open up on both of you."

Ella began to scream wildly, but there was nothing I could do. It was open the car door or risk getting us shot. Jimmy D pulled Ella out of the car and two of the gang bangers that were in his Lincoln pushed her into the back seat. Jimmy D put his pistol to my forehead.

"Bang, bang," he said, laughing. "Now I'm gonna adjust your junk so you won't be fuckin' around with what's mine, that white bitch. She's my property."

And with that, he pressed the gun between my legs. Just at that moment, one of Jimmy's boys yelled, "Cops! Cops! We gotta go, Jimmy."

Still, Jimmy thought he had enough time to blow off my penis, but I twisted away and the bullet went into my right thigh. He slammed the butt of a Saturday night special into my forehead.

"Bye fuck face."

I blacked out. I only survived because the cops found me and brought me to the hospital on DeKalb Avenue. The gun shot missed my femoral artery, but did some damage to the sciatic nerve. I woke up with my mother, red-eyed and sniffling into a tissue next to my bed.

"Giovanni, what happened?" And I told her the story of Jimmy D and Ella.

"No good comes from outside our people, Giovanni. When are you going to learn? *E' una cosa orribile. Un peccato, figlio mio, un peccato.*"

I was in that hospitable bed for nearly two weeks

before I could attempt to walk. Then two more weeks in therapy in the hospital as they monitored my progress. Finally, on Christmas Day, my mother and brothers came to take me home. And that is where I am today. I gave up my apartment in Bay Ridge. I left my job with the Department of Social Services. I am back with the family. Doing good, it seems, is the furthest thing from my mind these days.

My mother reminds me, "Remember when things were bad here and I sent you and your cousin 'to live with nonno and nonna in Bay Ridge? Well, we don't even know where Gino is or what happened to him. Things are bad for you this time and you must stay here in the bosom of your family. Remember Gianni, *la famiglia e' tutto. Era sempre cosi, figlio mio. Sempre cosi. Ti ricordi le parole di tuo padre? Chi non rispetta la sua famiglia, non rispetta se stesso."* Mamma said that the family is everything and that it had always been that way. She asked me if I remember what Papa used to say, "Whoever doesn't respect his family, doesn't respect himself."

And I began to see the truth of how my

adolescence and adult life was one long estrangement from my family; not in the sense of ignoring them or not loving them, but in the sense of not understanding what they were about and why they were the way they were. Family is life for an Italian, doubly so for a Sicilian. And respecting the family is everything. So began my change.

CHAPTER FOUR:
A Mix of Misery and Bliss

The car ride to Harlem was the longest half hour of my life. During it, Jimmy had my head pressed to his crotch, and as he stroked my hair, he said, "You're back with your Jimmy, woman. This time we livin' the high life. No more whorin' for you. You just my special girl. Now pucker those special lips of yours." And with that he began to unzip his pants. I was saved from that when the Navigator hit a pot hole and my forehead smashed into Jimmy's crotch.

"Ooh, bitch! Why you wanna do that for?" He raised his hand to me, but then said, "No, this ain't the old beatin' bitches Jimmy. That's not what I'm about. I'm about good sex, good dope, good champagne, a good crib. I've got the scratch now little mama. We're gonna live high."

And so he left me alone to think about how low I'd just fallen, how all the work I did on myself might be for nothing. It was almost too much to bear, but I knew I couldn't let Jimmy see me as weak. He'd have me whoring on the streets of Manhattan in no time. I became more miserable with each city street we passed on our way to Harlem. The Navigator stopped at Lenox and East 110th Street, right at the north end of Central Park. That's where Jimmy and his posse got out. They had me boxed in in case I tried to run for it: Jimmy in front and one of his men on either side and in back of me. I was too tired anyway. Jimmy could've just said "Follow me" and I would have. I needed rest and time to think. I was determined not to fall back into the servitude that had only ended the summer before.

"The girl needs to rest, needs her beauty sleep, ya know? Jax show her to her room."

And his henchman opened the door to a room I can only describe as Jimmy's dream of a high-priced hooker's bedroom: black satin and gold sheets, pillow cases and shams on a king-size bed with a mirror over it. There was plush, white, wall-to-wall carpeting. All the light switches had dimmers. The curtains were black damask. This was to be the playpen for Jimmy and me. But I was determined to keep him from being alone with me in the room, didn't want his body near mine ever again. The car ride uptown reminded me of how free I had finally felt and of how disgustingly degraded I felt around Jimmy.

My life done changed. I'm not runnin' *putas* anymore. I'm workin with *mi corro*, guys jus' like me. We come together and workin' for a big playah in NYC. Not sure who it is, but damn sure he made my life a lot better. Got this from a guy who tol' me a big shot who moved tons of *llello* liked my style and had steady work for me if I could get a small posse together. So like I go to *La Niña*, my favorite hangout, *mi chinchorro*. I tell *mis brokis* we got work, and bang, I gotta crew of a dozen guys. Our thing is to run protection for the shipments that come from *la isla*, Puerto Rico. In return, we get a point from each shipment. Don't always know exactly how much that be, different each time, but we got ourselves a nice buildin' here jus' pass' the Park, you know. Lan'lor' be real nice to us. Three floors. My *brokis* got the first two floors. I got my personal floor, number three, with a master bedroom for me and my *chilla*. That be Ella. She lookin' good now. I got it decorated nice, too. King size bed. Satin sheets all black and gold. Mirror over the bed. Black curtains. White rug, deep as shit. Ya feet get bury isso deep. I'm movin' up in the world, jus' like *la familia de los morenos, los Jefferson en la tele*. Three Navigators parked outside. One I bought for cash. Nobody bother us. We on our way.

So, I let her sleep las' night. She was confused, didn't know what was happ'nin'. She'll be happy today when she see what we got together, here. No more stinkin' projects, piss all over the hallway, you know. She's a lot bettah these days, too. I been watchin' her since I foun' out she went to rehab. I always knew she my special one, *mi chilla, mi bebe.*

I ain' gonna treat her like Tony Montana treated Elvira. I gonna treat her right. She'll see who I am, a man who can make his own life, a good life, a good man. So I popped dat fat WOP meatball on the stoop. Ain' nothin'. Jus' work like every day work. Business. Business is what it is, yeah. No sin in dat.

I did my business and I got my woman back. Dat's who I am, a guy who gets what he want. Somebody on the way up for sure.

Jimmy's been out most of the day, and it's given me time to think. First of all and most important, I've got to get out of here. But where to go? I violated my rehab agreement. I was supposed to be back after Thanksgiving weekend, so they probably won't take me back. I can't go to Johnny's. Jimmy knows where that is. Maybe I can go to his mother's place. But how can I get there? I just don't know. Every time I think of Jimmy possessing me again, I want to scream. But if I did, I'd have him or his henchmen on me in a

New York minute. And I just can't bear the sight of them. The way they talk. The way the dress. The way they hold themselves. This is not a world I want to live in. My life is meant for something better.

Then he comes through the door. "Yo, Ella!" Watcha think? We got a invite to the big boss's place tonight. Wants to meet me. Says I been doin' a good job on security. So doll up woman. Make sure you look good like you can. Put on that little black dress I boughtcha. I'm on my mothafuckin' way to the top now! I jus' gotta get tight with the main guy, and I can keep climbin'. Ella, you make'm look twice. You one sweet melon!"

Jimmy and I and two of his posse met with his boss's crew in Red Hook. We got out of the Navigator and went into a minivan. Jimmy's posse were left behind. The boss's men drove. Finally, we got out…on President Street! I thought Jimmy was going to turn and run, but he couldn't. There were men everywhere, and they were all armed. The next thing I knew Jimmy was gone and Mrs. Rosso met me at the door. I could see someone sitting in an armchair not far from the table where the extended family had had Thanksgiving dinner. It was Johnny.

"I'd get up to kiss you Ella, but my leg is still pretty weak."

"Johnny, I thought I'd never see you again." I ran to him and kissed him on the lips.

"But Johnny?" Before I could ask more, Mrs. Rosso jumped in.

"The Gaetas next door hired Jimmy and his boys to do a little work for their family. That's how we found out that he had taken you. We put two and two together and figured he was the one that killed Rocco. The Gaetas have him now. Sorry you didn't have the chance to say goodbye to him."

"So, you're the big boss, Mrs. Rosso?"

"Call me, Isabella."

CHAPTER FIVE:
Welcome to the Family

Isabella Rosso handed Ella Winters a demitasse of expresso.

"Tell me a little bit about yourself?" Isabella Rosso said, her blue eyes locked on mine.

"What is it you want to know?"

"Oh, about your folks, where you grew up, you know, the basics."

"I grew up out on the Island. My mother died after she gave birth to me. My father hated me for it."

"Your mother, what was her name?"

"Frannie? I think it was. Frannie and I don't quite know the last name. He just never mentioned her by name after she died. He didn't want to speak her name to me. I know she had blond hair and blue eyes, at least I'm pretty certain. My father's hair is dark and his eyes are brown, and as you can see, my eyes are blue and my hair is blond, a bit like yours."

"Do you know how they met?" Isabella was quite curious.

"I can't say. I think her English wasn't perfect because when I made a mistake on a composition for English class, my father would look at the paper and say, 'Just like your mother. She couldn't spell either.'"

"You know I had a twin sister. She ran away from home when we were sixteen. I think that's your story, too, isn't it? My sister, Francesca, was headstrong and certain that she didn't want to be an Italian, a Sicilian, and she didn't want any part of our business. So she left. We never could find her, and we tried. Lord knows we tried," she said hanging her head and suppressing a tear.

"And?"

"And you look like her. In fact, look at yourself in the mirror and look at me. Do you notice any resemblance?"

Then I gasped. A strange feeling came over me. I don't know quite what it was. As if perhaps I was finding a part of me that I didn't know was missing.

The process had begun. Isabella Rosso had an intuition about Ella Winters. She suspected that Ella held the answer to what happened to her twin sister, Francesca. She enlisted the family lawyer to find out. Jerry Lucas, the lawyer, was good at tying up loose ends. That had been his job for the Rossos for many years. What he found out changed the lives of Ella Winters and Isabella Rosso.

One day Lucas visited the Winters Long Island home. "Mr. Winters? My name is Jerry Lucas. I am acting on behalf of an anonymous donor who would like to reward you for certain information."

"What information could I possibly have to offer?"

"Really, just confirmation of a few documents. I have here a copy of your marriage license to Francesca Rosso and a copy of a birth certificate for your daughter, Isabella Winters. Can you confirm these?"

"I…I…but why do you want this information? Why do you need my confirmation?"

"Let's just say this person, who wishes to remain anonymous, is interested in confirming these documents. In return, you receive a payment of $10,000. You agree not to pursue the identity of this donor in any fashion and, one more thing. I have in my possession a form notarizing the adoption of your adult daughter by my client. You are not to make contact with your daughter who is now legally in her majority. Is that understood? I want to be very clear that there will be consequences if you break this agreement."

"I understand. How is she? I haven't seen her

since she was a high school student. I know I've neglected her. Tell her I'm sorry."

"Good day Mr. Winters. You will not see me again, nor speak of this meeting to anyone, please."

And so, Jerry Lucas, ne Luchesi, told this all to my aunt, Isabella Rosso. I took back my birth name of Isabella and adopted the surname of Rosso. Because there are now two Isabella Rossos in our family, the Rossos still call me Ella. It's easier that way. I am now part of the family. Isabella believes her sister, my mother, Francesca Rosso, lost her way when she left the family, but eventually realized her loss, so she named me after her twin to remember who she was and where she came from. This makes my relationship to Johnny cousin to cousin, so Isabella has made it clear that it goes no further than love for family. This removes the anxiety I had about my relationship to Johnny, but I think Johnny is disappointed. I think he was hoping we'd get together, but even if it hadn't happened that I was his blood, I'm pretty certain I would not have wanted that kind of relationship with Johnny. This way, I would never have to tell him that.

"Ella, my darling, there's so much I have to teach you," Isabella said as she gently drew me to her in a motherly hug. "I have had the good fortune to give birth to three sons, but I finally have the daughter my heart has longed for." And thus began my education in *la storia della famiglia Rosso,* a noble family of Altavilla, near present day Palermo, with records dating from the Middle Ages. It would continue with my trip to Sicily that winter.

It was *un viaggio solo.* Isabella signed me up for a month of Italian in Rome, and I learned more than language as I walked the streets of the Eternal City. In my soul, I felt a growing sense that I belonged, that this was part of who I am. That my family, my blood is mingled with the ancient streets of the city even though my Rosso family is Sicilian. As nobility, they must have trod these avenues, must have known the ins and outs of Italy's principal city and of the Papacy, enclosed as it is within Roman boundaries. During my

month in Rome, I visited the Catacombs, the
Coliseum, the Spanish Steps, the Trevi Fountain, the
Vatican, every famous landmark of the city. I spent
time in Felltrinelli, finding simple children's books in
Italian that I could read and understand, buying
histories of Italy, reading Ovid and Dante in
translation, taking the books to La Tassa d'Oro near
the Pantheon. There I would have a coffee and walk
out into the warm sun of the early spring afternoon to
the Piazza Navona, sit near the Fontana dei Quattro
Fiumi, and watch the passing parade: tourists asking
for directions, well dressed men rushing towards their
offices, old couples holding hands, fashionable young
mothers pushing strollers. What a sense of life being
lived! How beautifully the men and the women
dressed! There was a sense of pride in being a *citadino*,
a citizen of this wonderful city, that was nearly
palpable.

I was smitten.

I travelled down the peninsula by train, stopping
off in Pompei, in Paestum; taking a ferry from Naples
to Ischia and Capri; walking the hills of Tramonti,

Amalfi, and Positano. I stayed overnight in Sorrento, ate dinner under a glorious starry sky at a fish restaurant by a small harbor. The train stopped at the end of the peninsula, Villa San Giovanni. A few cars boarded the ferry, and we crossed the straits of Messina. My guide book on Sicily said that the whirlpool Charybdis, located in the Straits of Messina, was one of the dangers that Odysseus had to pass by with his men. I stood on the top deck of the ferry, craning my neck to get a look at this famous whirlpool from antiquity, but the ferry moved past it before I could really see anything. Still, I felt totally immersed in the timelessness of Italy. There was a lesson everywhere I went and I was an eager student.

When I reached Palermo, I was dead tired, but I couldn't sleep because a small delegation of about fifteen Rossos and assorted in-laws were there to meet me at the station. Isabella had let them know which train I would be on and when it would arrive. There followed hundreds of hugs and kisses. I was a part of a large family. I wasn't alone in this world. I finally felt what it was to have people in your corner just because you're you, because you are from the same wellspring of life. Though few of my Sicilian relatives spoke English, we communicated through touch, through gesture, and through a sense that we belonged to each other. I couldn't stop crying. I couldn't stop smiling. I couldn't stop my heart from spilling out into the warm spring air of the city.

The week that followed was a continuous lesson in family, history, geography, archaeology, cuisine, and language. On the island, I met Rossos in nearly every town, not just Altavilla. I was treated with love and affection and I returned the same. It wasn't just the people. I loved the sea, the ancient crumbling ruins that dotted the interior, the beauty of Taormina, the majesty of Etna, the Arab flavor of the Mediterranean west coast and the Greek flavor of the Ionian east coast. If I were to have an origin story, this was the place I would want it to start. Funny, I didn't even think of the other half of me, the Winters half. That was probably northern European, though my father considered himself a New Yorker, and nothing more. That was the beginning and end of the story for him. But my story was much larger, much greater, and if only half of me was Sicilian, then that half would have to stretch to make a whole. I was in love with the person I knew myself to be. I wasn't a junkie girl from Long Island any longer. As I boarded the flight from Palermo back to New York, I knew I was a strong Sicilian-American woman with a family behind her.

Isabella took me on a tour of Saks Fifth Avenue in midtown Manhattan. She pointed out the designers she was attracted to and who she thought designed for a woman of substance. She dressed almost exclusively in Eileen Fisher these days. She said her clothes spoke of elegance and command; they were right for a woman of her age. For me, she pointed to different designers: the Italians like Gucci, Prada and the rest. She said I had to choose carefully so I didn't go overboard. DKNY was mostly reliable. Dior was always a good choice. When I looked at the prices, I had to blink! I had never spent a thousand dollars for a pair of shoes or a simple dress.

"You are on a different social level now, *tesoro mio*. How you choose to dress and how you carry yourself are of utmost importance. That is why we are on this shopping trip. It is part of your education as a woman of this family."

I just looked at her and gave her a kiss on the cheek. "Thank you, Isabella. I mean *grazie mamma*." And at those last words, Isabella smiled at me. This is what she wanted, for me to see her as my mother, to treat me as her daughter. And if this wise and strong woman felt that way about me, who was I to deny her? After all, I had never had a mother, never known what it was to share a mother's love. Perhaps now I would, even though I was an adult.

"By the way, a smart woman chooses clothing that will last and will always be in fashion. In that way, she can buy expensive pieces because she will have them for a long time. She does not need closets full of dresses, shoes and handbags. One closet will do for all if she chooses wisely. *Va bene?*"

"*Si, ti capisco, mamma.*"

61

Within a single year, my life had changed completely. I could never have anticipated this outcome, this new role I was to play. I could never have foreseen that I would find the essential part of me I was missing. In my childhood sadness, I felt the need for love and care, but didn't receive either. In my teenage years, I wanted intimacy, but only received sexual intimacy without the love necessary to make it meaningful. Now, as a young woman, I am being paid back all the love that is owed me. What a wonderful feeling! But there was darkness even as the light poured through my soul. I was shortly to learn how the Rossos rose to their standard of living.

CHAPTER SIX:
La Cosa Nostra

Large numbers of Italian immigrants came to America during the late nineteenth century to early twentieth – the textbooks frame it as 1890 to 1920. By 1920, there were four million Italians, making up about ten percent of the immigrant population. They were mostly southern Italians of little means. They were Catholic and they were non-English speaking. They were used to having fathers and sons and mothers and daughters working alongside one another in agriculture and trade. Yet they were not all the same.

In such a large immigrant group, there were

those, Sicilians for example, who had ties to groups in their homeland whose function changed in America. The origin of the Sicilian Mafia was in clans and families who protected themselves against outside forces, including other Sicilians. Eventually, these families formed small armies that shook down landowners for protection money, and adjudicated disputes in their areas of influence according to their own laws. It was a culture of initiation, secrecy and intimidation. These qualities persisted in the American Mafia, La Cosa Nostra, but its sphere of influence had its beginnings in the Italian immigrant ghettos, and eventually extended to the American underworld, taking off during Prohibition. Such were the Rossos, my family.

Isabella was a Rosso by birth and she married a Rosso, a third cousin. In Italian culture, this was not uncommon. She grew up understanding that the family business was largely illegal and that sometimes the men of the family did things that were just evil: murder and intimidation of enemies and innocents.

While her great-grandfather and grandfather were Mafiosi, her husband, Vittorio, never was initiated into that secret society despite the fact that his older brothers were. His father wanted an American son, one who succeeded by virtue of his talent and connections in the larger society, not just in the smaller circle of Sicilian men of honor.

Vittorio Rosso became a tax lawyer and a very good one. He began by handling his father's legal affairs. He was deliberately kept away from the illegal part of the business. Through Vittorio's cleverness, the family prospered. While Isabella understood herself to be part of a family that did business in both worlds, she became much more comfortable when, at Vittorio's insistence, the family began to invest a lot in its legal businesses like transportation, carting, importing, and construction. It was her husband's death at the hands of a Crip gunman, who mistook the mild-mannered Vittorio for a soldier in a different Mafia family, that created the occasion for Isabella's rise to her position of power within the family. She bought out the interests of Vittorio's older brothers and sisters. They never understood Vittorio's desire "to go legit," and they resented the special role their father had chosen for him, the American son. Vittorio's siblings chose to remain in the underworld of fear, intimidation, and illegal activities while Isabella framed a new definition of the Rosso family business. I am lucky to become part of the family and of Rosso Industries as it is now, totally above board. Isabella found out who had shot Johnny by asking her oldest sons to contact the Gaetas, who she suspected of some involvement. Even then, she didn't take retribution, but rather left that to the Gaeta family. It was their *soldato*, Rocco La Paglia, Jimmy D had killed last Thanksgiving.

One evening, Isabella summoned me for a talk about business. "For years, we have been importing olive oil from Tuscany and selling it under the brand name of *Olio Buono*. It is good oil. We own several groves in the Tuscan countryside. Our business has been profitable, but in the past few years, with one thing and another, production has fallen, and so have our profits. I'd like you to take a trip to our suppliers and try to figure out how we can create a more profitable business."

"Okay, Mamma. I'll leave right away."

"Use our travel agency. They'll get you a good seat on Alitalia. I'll give you a list of people to consult when you get there."

I flew into Florence and stayed a few days, making my acquaintance with the David at the Accademia di Belle Arti, and the statues in the Piazza della Signoria in front of the Palazzo Vecchio, the Fountain of Neptune, the Rape of the Sabine Women, and the reproduction of the David at the entrance to the Palazzo. I had no time for the Uffizi because I wanted to get on the Chiantigiana road the next day. It goes from Florence to Siena. This was the prime region in Tuscany for both chianti and olive oil. That noon, in front of the cathedral in Siena, I was to meet Santo d'Onofrio, our orchard manager, a slender gray haired man in his sixties. He was dressed in dark slacks, loafers, a cream-colored silk shirt and a tan camel's hair jacket. He was well groomed and he spoke English well, laced with Italian.

"*Signorina Rosso?*"

"*Sì, sono io. lei dev'essere il dottor D'Onofrio. Piacere di conoscerla, dottore!*" (Yes, that's me. You must be Dr. D'Onofrio. Pleased to meet you doctor.)

"*Sì sì, appunto* (Exactly). You are right and you are lovely. *Il piacere 'e mio.. .Al suo servizio*" (The pleasure is mine. At your service.).

I knew this immediate flattery was standard operating procedure with Italian men interacting with *straniere*, foreign women, particularly Americans. Still, it made me smile. "Why thank you for the compliment. You are certainly a sharp dresser, *Dottore.*"

"Sharp? *Che vuol'dire?*"

"Stylish, *a la moda, no?*"

"Ah, I see. You compliment my clothes, but not me. How sad then to be an old man as I am."

This playful bantering with the hint of sexual innuendo in every rejoinder reminded me of the delight Italians take in *fare la bella figura*, looking good to others in public, and acting the part as well, implying that they knew themselves unavoidably attractive to members of the opposite sex.

"If I may, *Signorina*, I know a very good restaurant not far from here. The food is simple, but honest. I hope you will like it."

It was more than simple and better than delicious. The Dottore plied me with wine, both red and white, but I managed to focus on business while showing my enthusiasm by continually raising the wine glass to my lips, taking infinitely small sips each time I did.

"The orchards are not producing so much these past years, Signorina. I know your mother must be disappointed."

"No, I wouldn't say disappointed. She knows you do your best for her. I would say she is looking to supplement our production with that of another maker. And so, because you are a good friend of many years, she asks you through me to find a second supplier for olive oil."

"You know I did not know your mother had a daughter. I thought only the three boys. But I can see, she has not only a daughter, but a good businesswoman."

"Flattery, my good *dottore*, may get you somewhere, but not on this trip." I raised my eyebrow just a bit as if to imply his seductive techniques were having the effect he desired. "I really need to nail down a second supplier."

"*Cos' `e* 'nail down' ? *Un nail e' un chiodo, no?*"

"*Forse significa 'abbiamo bisogno di ottenere un secondo fornitore sicuro.'*" (Perhaps 'We need to obtain securely a second supplier.').

"*Ho capito.*"

"*E poi?*"

"Well, I think you need to go south to the toe of

the boot of Italia, perhaps Calabria. I have one friend who can show you some orchards. His name is Abraham Aiello."

So I drove down to Calabria in a rented four door Smart sedan, competing with the wind and rain as I drove over the Apennines, and with the Italian drivers, who delighted in splashing my windshield as they passed me at lightning speed. I deliberately took the A1, an additional two hours, because I wanted to see a bit of the Adriatic Coast. After a long day's drive, I found myself in Reggio Calabria, where I met Aiello at his neighborhood bar on Giudecca Street, a street which referred back to the presence of the Jewish community in Reggio. It was in this part of the city that the first Hebrew Bible was printed in 1475. Aiello was about d'Onofrio's age, in his sixties, though he looked to have had a harder life. Lines on his forehead paired with the sorrow in his eyes spoke of events best forgotten. I surmised he must have lost family under Mussolini.

"Good afternoon, Miss Rosso. I hope the drive wasn't too taxing."

Aiello's English was excellent, I would find. He knew precisely the right word to use.

"Unfortunately, it was just that, Signore Aiello. I wonder if we could conduct our business after dinner this evening."

"That would be fine, but if you would permit me, I would like to escort you to dinner at the Ristorante Gala'. It is in your hotel, the Excelsior, on the fifth floor and affords a wonderful vista of the Straits of Messina."

"That would be lovely, Signore. Shall we say 7:30?"

"Very good. I shall knock on your hotel room door at 7:30."

Abraham Aiello was as good as his word. He knocked on my hotel room door precisely at 7:30. Signore Aiello represented Old World charm and manners. Women were to be escorted. Doors were to be opened for them, arrangements to be made on their behalf, choices suggested for their consideration.

I admit that I liked it, especially by comparison to the don juanism of d'Onofrio.

"Miss Rosso, my name is Abraham. Do you know what that represents? Especially in this country?"

"Abraham...hmmm...Abraham Lincoln, perhaps our greatest president, but then Abraham of the Old Testament, a Jewish name..."

"Precisely. It is as a Jew I have both prospered and suffered in this country, yet I would never leave it. We Jews have wandered the earth, looking for a place to call our own. Many now call Israel home, but for the Jews of Italy, our fortunes and fates have been part of Italian history. We are as Italian as any Roman or Tuscan. Yet we still live apart in many ways, some by choice, others not."

"Are you referring to the years under fascism when Mussolini followed Hitler's policy on Jews?"

"Yes, under him, the *Manifesto della Razza* became law in 1938. It stripped Jews of their citizenship and professional standing. Yet despite the brutality to Jews under fascism and Nazism, Italy had the second highest rate of survival for Jews during this period. Only Denmark did a better job of protecting her Jews. We were here before Rome was founded. Our history in this country has had many periods of discrimination and expulsion. On the other hand, Spanish Jews found refuge in this country when they were expelled from Spain. So, a very checkered past, but still we Jews cling to our Italian selves, and in an age when culture has superseded religion, many of us feel ourselves first Italians and second Jews. I tell you all this because I want you to know the man you are dealing with, that is, if we do conclude a business partnership."

Aiello drove me to his orchards the next day. I tasted the 'green gold' that was his first pressing. It was delicious. Where once oil from southern Italy was of low quality, today, in orchards like Aiello's, it is award winning oil. Aiello's oil was extracted from organically farmed olives, hand-picked from his orchards in Cosenza. The aroma of the oil is strong, round, and I could taste tomato, sage, and mint in it. Aiello smiled when I told him this. "Not everyone picks up those tastes the first time. Excellent, Miss Rosso. *Ottimo!*" It had a sweet almond finish. I loved it, and I became a student of olive oil on that visit to Reggio Calabria.

Aiello and I had a picnic Italian style at his orchards. We weren't alone. His wife and two married daughters with their assorted toddlers came to join us. His eldest son came in from the orchards to sit under a sun umbrella and uncork bottles of Savuto, a rich red from the Cosenza area. "You know, Miss Rosso, the Greeks loved the wine from this area. The old name for our land was Enotria, the land of wines. People think that Italian wine begins and ends in Tuscany. Not true, Miss Rosso. Not true!"

Aiello smiled at me as he said this, a smile rich in love and satisfied with life, a smile from a patriarch of a successful clan. This was Abraham Aiello.

We drew up a contract the next day. "In the old days, men shook hands on a deal. One's word was one's bond. That is no longer true, Miss Rosso. However, I feel that I could have done that with you. I trust you."

"*Anch'io mi fido di lei, Signore Aiello.*" (I also trust you, Sr. Aiello.)

We parted as friends and business associates. The glow of my interaction with the Aiellos sustained me all the way back to President Street. My first big deal looked like a good one. Mama was happy. I was happy.

CHAPTER SEVEN:
The Lesson

The redhead and I are at Central Park. We are strolling through the park, delighting in the laughter of the young. They are everywhere: gawking at the animals in the zoo, flying frisbees and kicking soccer balls in the Sheep Meadow; playing guitar and singing Beatles' songs at Strawberry Fields; sailing boats on the lake. Suddenly the redhead stops walking and stands statue still, listening for a sound I cannot hear. She jumps into the lake and begins swimming. I run behind her, but dare not jump in. The weather is chilly and a wind is blowing trash and leaves through the fall air.

I want to call out to her, but I cannot.

I awoke. The dreams continued even though my situation was very different these days. I might be called a semi-invalid. The bullet that just missed the femoral artery did enough nerve damage to make walking difficult for me. I used a cane. I was largely housebound. I spent my days watching. I watched my brothers, Gildo and Gennaro, as they wasted the possibilities of each day, neither one with ambition, content to be part of the family and do Mamma's bidding. I watched Ella, now reborn as Isabella Rosso, take center place in Mamma's heart. And I think I could have had her for nothing when she was down and out on junk. Now that I want her, I can never have her. She went from my client, to my cousin and then my sister. And I thought some more, what was it that I could do in this world? My Masters in Social Work was of no interest to me now. I was no longer a social worker. I refused to become a recluse, a shut in, an object of sympathy for others. I needed to walk into the world again. But how? This question occupied my waking hours; its answer eluded me. But I had to find an answer or I would lose any spark of life within me.

So, I read the papers, watched CNN, kept myself

aware of the political scene, the economy, international relations, and then what? There was only so much rehashing of news one could share with others if he himself did not make any news of his own. Life was hard, yes it was. Yet I had my life and, as far as I knew, Jimmy D didn't have his. I don't know what the Gaetas did with him. I don't want to know.

Everyone needs a little danger in his life. That's why I started betting. I bet on things I knew pretty well. I had always been a sports fan, so I bet the Knicks, the Mets and the Giants, my teams. Sometimes I bet with them and sometimes against. I limited myself, a hundred dollars a week. I kept records. So far, I was a thousand to the good. Being from the family I was from, I had no trouble finding a reliable bookie. No one was going to lay heavy vigorish on a Rosso. I guess that was one good thing I got from our illegal past, respect in a certain part of society, the part that made its money with no thought of paying taxes on it.

Then one day I turned off the television and kept

my money in my wallet, no more gambling. A change was bound to come.

Mamma said I should get out more. But limping through the neighborhood and all those eyes watching poor gimpy me made me angry. I could drive, but I'd sold my Prius after I got out of the hospital. Still I needed a car so that I could get around without eyes all over me. I bought an old VW Bug. I drove it to the gym I joined, a twenty-four hour deal; I could go any time of day. I hired a trainer to work with me, modifying exercises because of my leg. It was three months later, and I could see some results. My arms were strong and my waist was narrow. My limp was even a little better. Thank God I decided to join a gym! I had been getting a roll of fat around the middle and my face was becoming soft and featureless.

One day I was at the gym when this little Asian guy was working out with some light weights, doing very slow repetitions, and extending his arms and legs to their limit. This started to bother one of the steroid bozos who work out there.

"Hey, Chink! Let's move it, hunh? I ain't got all day."

The Asian guy didn't answer.

"Hey fuckface! Ain'chu heard me?"

"I am not Chinese, and my name is not fuckface. I will continue my exercises. You will have to wait your turn."

With that, 'roid boy grabbed the Asian by the shoulders and spun him around. He cocked his right hand back ready to punch. As the punch moved toward the smaller man, he turned his body and grabbed the extended arm of his attacker while moving his hands so quickly that I couldn't follow. The oaf fell in a heap. The Asian helped him up, and looked at him not in triumph, but as another pilgrim on a journey, perhaps many steps behind his own.

"Now I will continue my exercises," said my future sen-sei.

That was my first lesson in aikido with Kobayashi Sen-Sei, learning to see and confront darkness without harming the one who lives in its shadow. I started on a path that began as physical training. It eventually became a spiritual practice centered around the art of peace. Aikido is a way of the warrior founded on preserving a peaceful universe, taking care of all that lives, doing as much as one can to practice virtue and obtain knowledge.

That was the start of the change in me. I was no longer worried about my path in life because aikido was teaching me the path I must follow. My waking hours were devoted to practice and study. I enrolled in an intensive Japanese course, so that I could speak to my master better and understand his culture. As soon as I started studying, I recognized that the journey would be life-long. There was so much to learn and I was just at the beginning. I was fortunate, too because Kobayashi Sen-Sei did not usually take students as old as I was, in my late twenties, but my enthusiasm won him over. In this way, my life transformed. I could never have foreseen such a change, but there it was, and I was the better for it.

One morning, having practiced *misogi*, purifying

myself with a cold water bath while meditating on the life force within me, I stepped into the living room to find Ella there, waiting for me, just back from her trip to Italy.

"Hi, Ella, Mamma told me you had a successful trip to the south of Italy, negotiating for more olive oil importing. Congratulations!"

"Thanks, Johnny. Johnny, I'd like to say something to you. I realize that things have changed because of me. If I have hurt you in any way, I mean, if you think I am coming between you and Mamma, I want you to know that I would never try to take your place in your mother's heart."

"Thanks, Ella. The truth is that I am happy to have you as my sister even though I have come to love you in a different way: you must already know that. But I can change, too. And I have to for both our sakes. You know for a while after the shooting, I had no idea what to do. Then, serendipity! I met my future by chance in the form of a small old Japanese man at the local twenty-four hour fitness gym. I am now a student of aikido, his student, Kobayashi Sen-Sei's student."

"Aikido is a martial art, right? So how does it make a life for you?"

"In many ways. First of all, it centers me, gives me a sense of purpose. It creates the desire to learn, to study and for a good reason: to live in this world harmoniously with myself and with others. In a way, it's a logical next step from my impulse to serve others, that same impulse that pushed me into social work."

"I see, but what about the practical need to make a living?"

"I have enough saved for five years of study, study I hope to do in Japan. I'll go there when Kobayashi Sen-Sei returns next month. After that, we'll see where I am in life."

"Your leg doesn't stop you from practicing a martial art?"

"No, it's just a small stone on the path I have

taken. As I practice aikido, it seems less and less of a problem."

Ella drew near me and opened her arms. Perhaps for the last time I held her as if she were mine, not my sister, but my lover. I kissed her on the cheek and let go. I was letting go the first part of my life. The next part was to come and it made me eager to start.

CHAPTER EIGHT:
The Making of a Hitman

"Bring the Spik in," Crazy Bobby Gaeta ordered.

Head down, eyes down. Jimmy D shuffled in.

"Hey, douche bag. You did exactly what we wanted. Rocco was skimming and we had to get rid of him, but we didn't want any heat. So, you got the hit."

At that Jimmy D looked at Bobby. He had no idea which way was down and which up. He didn't know who was calling the shots. He just knew he wasn't.

"Everything's just okay. Smile, asshole. This is the first day of the rest of your life and we got plans

87

for you."

"But.."

"Fuck but, amigo. Here's what's gonna happen. You're goin' upstate, to Woodstock. Yeah, I like that irony, all peace and love, but you're gonna be our hitman, unnerstan'?"

Jimmy said nothing, but he was all ears.

"Yeah, the boys gonna take you upstate. We gotchu a little house and we gonna keep you alive, give you a little mad money. When we want a hit, we give you a bump, a grand a head. How's that?"

"You do this for me, Mr. Gaeta?"

"Yeah, call it multicultural cooperation, *mi hermano.*"

So that was the beginning of Jimmy D's new life. He became a resident of a small rural town that still carried the vibe of the 1969 music festival known the world over. Maybe he'd rub shoulders with movie stars, musicians and politicians. Who could tell?

Jimmy was moved into a cedar-shingled one story home in Willow, about seven miles from Woodstock on Route 212. It was close to the Phoenicia Forest, out in the country, where Jimmy'd never spent a day in his life. For the first two weeks, he was miserable. The Gaetas had eyes on him during this time, so he didn't try to run. He had no car; he hitched into Woodstock when he could. He would go to the Dunkin' Donuts and sit with a coffee and a donut for an hour or two and hope for the rich and famous, who sometimes came up from the city, to walk through the door. But Jimmy just saw average Joes and Janes, people no one knew but their families, friends and employers. When he could sit and dawdle no longer, he hitched back to the house for lunch; a Gaeta minder was always there to ask him where he'd been.

In the afternoon, he took to walking the trails in the woods. After, he'd come back and boil some water, then throw two packets of ramen noodles in it with an egg. This was his dinner. Boredom drove him to sleep by nine o'clock; he was up with the dawn.

This routine lasted a month and Jimmy thought he'd go crazy from the monotony. Finally, the minders left with instructions for Jimmy to work on his trade. Along with the written note was a Colt Model 1911 and cartons of 22 caliber bullets.

"There are cans and bottles in the garage. Practice on them," the note read. "When we need you, you better make your first shot count or else we'll cancel our investment in you."

Practice Jimmy did. He got very good, and since he wasn't drinking or using, his hand was steady and his aim was true. He started to work on his physique. He made a barbell by sinking cement into two paint cans and attaching each one to the end of a metal pole. Before breakfast, he ran the forest trail for a mile out and back, and then he did pushups, sit-ups and jumping jacks in sets of three. Exercise was followed by a breakfast of oatmeal, walnuts, and raisins with black coffee. He started to learn to cook some simple meals for lunch and dinner: chicken soup, chili, beef stew. The Gaetas gave him an allowance of five hundred dollars a month, and they covered all the expenses of the house: heat, trash, electric, and phone, but no internet or TV for Jimmy. He had to make do with entertaining himself. He took to hitching to the town library and sitting for hours with books on health, nutrition, and cooking. He wrote down recipes, then went to the local supermarket to buy ingredients to try them out.

Jimmy didn't know it, but he was changing, changing like a snake shedding its skin. It would still be a snake, but it would have new skin. Part of the change was in his way of talking to people. In the city, he'd affected a heavy Puerto Rican gangsta jargon; this immediately got him street cred with those like him, and scared the Anglos and other non-Latinos he dealt with daily. But Jimmy also knew how to "talk right." As a pimp, he needed to be smooth with white Johns, not threatening; he'd save that part for the girls. So, Jimmy was master of two ways of talking, and it was the smoother, non-threatening one that served him well in Woodstock. That change didn't even cross Jimmy's mind. It was just natural.

Life in upstate New York, away from the city,

was slower and less interesting for Jimmy. It made him restless, looking for something more. He found out that a private liberal arts college, mostly attended by wealthy kids, had a program for low income students. The college was about a half hour from where Jimmy now lived. One day he showed up at the college, found out who was administering the program, and talked his way into late enrollment. He also talked the program into loaning him a computer so he could do his course work online. The program paid for installation and monthly fees as well. Jimmy was now on the internet, where his primary and abiding interest was surfing Ella and Johnny.

Aside from pornography and sports, there wasn't a lot on the internet to interest Jimmy. He again grew restless, antsy, unable to concentrate on the composition course he was taking online. He realized what it was. He needed a woman. The Gaetas had been very specific in telling him that he wasn't to have contact with townspeople other than a hello, but the urge was very strong, so Jimmy disobeyed and started trolling singles websites for women in the area. That's how he found Star Phillips, a single mother of two, living a mile from town. Her post said she was looking for a lasting relationship. They emailed back and forth a few times, and then Jimmy knocked on her door one day.

"Hi, I'm Jimmy Diamond…moved up here a couple of months ago…just up the road towards Willow. I was surfing the net, and well… we found each other, didn't we? Can I come in?"

Star blushed, but she was a desperate woman, thirty-five with no prospects and two children of middle school age, Maisie and Davie, who occupied her time day and night. Jimmy looked good to her.

Soon after Jimmy took up with Star, he got another weapon and another note from the Gaetas.

"Here's a hunting rifle with a good scope on it. Practice from at least the length of a football field. Use bigger targets like plastic buckets in bright colors and when you get good, plastic buckets that blend in with the trees and plants around your place. Oh yeah, and the rifle uses 22s, too, just like the pistol we gave you. We don't want you to get caught on your first job because you got some fancy gun or rifle. You gotta learn to blend in when you do work for us. We got a job for you 'round Christmas, so practice."

Jimmy and Star were doing well together. She'd cook for him after she put her kids to bed. He'd spend the night and then leave before they woke up. But pretty soon he stayed later. As the days went by, he found himself mostly at her place. He even moved a suitcase full of clothes over. He went back to his place just to check in, catch up on his online class, and go into the woods to shoot. Christmas was drawing near. Life wasn't so bad.

The day came, the day before Christmas Eve. He was building a snow man with Star's kids in her front yard. It had snowed during the night, and the ground was covered with six inches of fresh whiteness. For Jimmy, it made everything clean and new again. That afternoon, he walked through the snow to his house and found a note waiting for him. "Pack a bag and be ready. We'll pick you up at six o'clock tonight."

Back at Star's, over dinner, Maisie asked, "Jimmy, will you be our Santa?"

"Santa will come himself, he doesn't need me," he answered, but he could barely get out the words. He swallowed hard. "He'll be here and I will too," he added, but without much conviction.

"Yeah, sure. Just like our real dad," Maisie said disheartedly.

Two Gaeta soldiers came at exactly six o'clock. They said nothing, merely opened the back door of the Caddy for Jimmy to get in. "Gotcha gun?" was the only question asked. The short nervous one Jimmy knew as Willy handed him a picture. "He lives in Queens. Ask for Arnold. If his wife answers, tell her it's a message from his friend, Bobby. He'll come quick. Pop him and leave. We'll be waiting a block away. Look for us. Oh, and use this," he said, throwing Jimmy a silencer for the pistol.

It was a very desultory crime, no passion, no reason given. Jimmy knocked on the door of a semi-detached brownstone in Astoria. An older woman with a worn out face answered the door. "Yes?"

"Is Arnold in?"

"And who should I say is asking?"

"I have a message from his friend, Bobby."

"Wait here."

Within a minute, a short, bald man wearing a cardigan sweater and a pair of black rimmed glasses with Coke bottle lenses shuffled to the door.

"You gotta message from Bobby?"

"Arnold?"

"Yeah, who else?"

Jimmy pulled the Colt out of his coat. He had put a silencer on it as instructed. He shot Arnold once in the chest and once between the eyes. Wordlessly, Arnold dissolved into a heap on his welcome mat. Jimmy turned and walked quickly away. He saw the Gaeta Caddy up ahead; he started sweating profusely, even though the temperature was below freezing. He got in the car.

"Go okay?"

"Yeah, Willy."

"Awright. We gonna take you with us just for the night. Awright wi' youse?" Willy liked to affect a strong Brooklyn accent when he was being a stock movie wise guy.

"Sure, Willy."

That night Jimmy slept in one of the Gallo's safe houses. Willy and Big Joey, his two minders, didn't seem to sleep at all. Jimmy later learned they had checked to make sure that Arnold was dead. They intercepted a police band bulletin detailing the shooting, then they double checked with Roger Maher, a cop on their payroll for Queens.

"Dead as a doornail," Maher reported.

They drove Joey back to Willow on Christmas Eve morning. Jimmy never knew anything about Arnold: who he was, why he was a target. Willy threw him an envelope just before the Caddy peeled out of his driveway. In it were ten crisp hundred dollar bills. Jimmy thought he could make Star's Christmas a little cheerier, even buy some toys for the kids.

ACCOUNTANT SHOT IN ASTORIA

Arnold Goldman, 69, an accountant who worked privately from his home in Astoria, Queens, was shot and killed Saturday. His wife, Rachel Goldman, found his body in the doorway of their home. Police said there was no evident motive for the crime although Goldman was alleged to have mob connections.

Star read the story in the local paper on Christmas morning. "See this Jimmy? Guy got shot in his own doorway. I'm not surprised. That city is a hell hole, as dangerous as ever." She showed Jimmy the article.

He couldn't get over it. His hit had made the

papers! He stuck out his chest just a little further, and then just as quickly drew it in; he felt remorse at his crime, which he had no reason to commit, as far as he knew. "It was different when I killed Rocco," he thought. Then he thought again, "Why? Why was it any different?"

"The only good thing that no good shit of a husband, my big rock star ex, did good was move us out of that city!" Star shook her head. "Murdered on his own doorstep!"

On New Year's Day, Jimmy was snuggling with Star in her bed, an empty champagne bottle on the night table, clothes strewn about the room.

Domestic bliss of a kind for Jimmy and Star. The kids had had a sleepover at one of their friend's homes. A pair of saintly parents had volunteered to take care of a half dozen kids besides their own, so that at least some could enjoy a proper New Year's Eve.

The call came at noon. "Pack a bag and bring the rifle. Be ready in an hour."

Jimmy had to do some tall explaining to Star as to why he was all of a sudden hurriedly dressing and walking back to his place. He got himself together just in time to meet the Caddy. This time Willie and Big Joey weren't there. It was a good looking young guy with blond hair slicked back under ounces of gel. "Get in, Jimmy," he said with a voice that knew its authority. We're going to the city. Your target is in a patrol car. Here's his picture, and don't tell me all cops look the same."

"A cop! I can't do it. Not that."

"You have no choice."

And he didn't. Blondie drove Jimmy to a corner building, and set him up on the second floor. Jimmy had a view of traffic in four directions.

"He'll be in a cruiser, coming into your sights in fifteen minutes. He's driving."

"How do you know?"

"He's our stooge. That's how. Bought and paid for. Now new rent is due."

"But why?"

"Haven't they trained you not to ask that question, Jimmy? Just shoot him. Shoot Michael Maher." And Jimmy did. Two shots to the head through the open window of the squad car. Maher was tossing a cigarette out the window when he was hit.

POLICEMEN SHOT IN BENSONHURST

At 4PM on New Year's Day, Sergeant Michael Maher was on routine patrol in the Bensonhurst district of Brooklyn when two shots rang out and killed him. "We are filled with sorrow for the Maher family. Sergeant Maher was a fifteen year veteran of the NYPD. His killer will be brought to justice, said spokesperson Jane Cleverly.

"Another news story about me," thought Jimmy. "Another thousand in the bank. I don't feel too good about the hit, but I don't feel bad about it either. I don't feel anything. It's a different world. Not my world. My world's here with Star and her kids."

Winter moved slowly into a muddy spring in Woodstock, and Jimmy became domestic. He swept the wooden floors of Star's bungalow. Outdoors, he raked the remaining leaves into huge flavescent piles. Then he picked up Maisie, who was nearly ten, and Davie, who was nine, and tossed them each into a pile of leaves, the children's cheeks red with excitement and the remaining bite of a winter wind. Smiles all around, including one large grin from Star, watching from the kitchen window. He hadn't heard from the Gaetas for three months, and he hoped that he wouldn't hear from them again though he knew he would. He tried to keep it all out of his mind. If it got really bad, he ran a few miles in the woods and came back to make love to Star in sweat and heat.

The call did come on a sunny April morning, crocuses peeking out on the front lawn, and a song bird or two making music for mating in the oaks behind Star's place. The same command in the note. The same hurry-up-and-get-ready. The same neutered, bloodless execution of a person Jimmy'd never met. Then back to a safe house for a night, and a drop off in town the next morning. Jimmy deliberately tried to forget everything he had to know to do the hit. He got good at making his mind blank right after the job. The Gaetas appreciated Jimmy's economy and lack of interest in anything but doing the gig and getting back home. Willy made a mental note that Jimmy was just about a husband to Star and a father to her kids. That could be of use one day.

CHAPTER NINE:
Aikido

For me, life in Japan was the exact same and the exact opposite of life in New York. There was the hustle and bustle of Tokyo: commuters squeezed into trains, coffee houses, restaurants, fast food places, bars. There was a business district, a red-light district, a restaurant district. All this reminded me of New York City. But then there were the Japanese. When they counted, they started with an open hand and then closed each finger. When they spoke, the verb was at the end of the sentence. When they interacted, no one said No. The sexes were segregated mostly, but came together in odd places like hot springs and bath houses. They loved western music and western movies. They imitated western fashion. Yet Japanese traditions such as koto music, Noh theater, kimonos, calligraphy and the Geisha of Kyoto represented the Japanese ideal.

Kobayashi Sen-Sei was from Nara in central Japan, an ancient imperial city, mentioned in the second oldest book of Japanese traditional history, the Nihon-shoki. Nara, the capital of Japan during the eighth century AD, was the principal conduit for Chinese culture entering Japan. The upper classes of Nara adopted Chinese Buddhism, and in general sought to imitate many aspects of Chinese culture, including works of art and literature. It is a city with Buddhist temples, Shinto shrines, the former imperial palace, and places of natural beauty. I couldn't get over the hundreds of sika deer walking around Nara Park. Once considered sacred, they were now regarded as national treasures. But all of this was just incidental to my purpose, which was to study with Kobayashi Sen-Sei.

In the foothills of Wakakusayama, a mountain

east of Nara Park, Kobayashi Sen-Sei had his dojo. I lived in a make shift dormitory behind the dojo along with two other students of the sen-sei. These were the chosen ones who would carry on the sen-sei's teaching. I only hoped that I might be among them, but I wasn't sure. I sometimes thought I was there as a novelty and a status symbol. To have a westerner seriously studying with you brought some cachet to a Japanese aikido master.

I was treated just like the other two disciples, who were both Japanese. We prepared the meals, cleaned the dojo, saw to the sen-sei's needs, rose at dawn every morning and ran barefoot through the streets, rain, snow or shine. My leg pained me most in the damp winter rain, but I learned that one of the virtues I had to cultivate was *gaman*, enduring the unendurable. This was a necessity for any serious student of aikido or for a student of any other Japanese martial art. Another value I learned was *giri,* a sense of duty far greater than its English translation. To practice *giri* was to sacrifice the self in devotion to one's superiors. These two martial virtues were ingrained in everything that I did every day. Without *gaman* and *giri*, there could be no learning and no practice.

I became accustomed to sitting in meditation with my haunches folded back on my calves, knees pointing forward, back straight, eyes closed, torso completely motionless, breath so quiet as to be inaudible. At first, it hurt! Oh did it hurt! But I fought through the pain. I accepted everything that the sen-sei taught me. I learned to understand in a visceral way without the need for constant praise or explanation.

One day, I sat kneeling before sen-sei, whose English was minimal, but to the point.

"Johnny. It...time."

"It is time, sen-sei?"

"Yes, you must to go back. You must to make a dojo and you must to teach."

"But I am still so inept. I lose so many bouts I enter."

"This not important. You know *kata*. You learned meaning of aikido. You ready."

"I will find it hard sen-sei. I will find it hard to leave your presence. You are the light that shines into my soul. How can I leave?"

"Not so. That light in all of us. Most never use. That is all. Go tomorrow."

"Yes, sen-sei, and thank..."

"Stop, unnecessary speak between teacher and student. What not speak is important. Pass on knowledge important."

"Yes, sen-sei."

And thus five years of my life, the five years I would always count as the best and deepest of my life, passed. I returned to New York City, to Brooklyn, a stranger in a land made strange from me by my total devotion to my life with Kobayashi Sen-Sei under Wakakusayama in Nara.

CHAPTER TEN:
Time and Change

Isabella Rosso and her adopted daughter were discussing the family business one evening. Ella was thinking of expansion, but that wasn't on Isabella's mind. For months, she had kept her physical condition secret, and because Ella was away on business much of the time, she never thought much about her mother's weight loss, gray pallor, and slow movements.

"Our balance sheet looks better and better, Mamma. If you're thinking about a new venture for Rosso International, the best time may be now."

"Perhaps, tesoro mio, but there is something of

greater importance we need to discuss."

"Oh, Johnny's return?"

"No, not that."

"Then expanding one of our existing businesses."

"Not that either."

"Then what?"

"It's time. Time for you to take charge of the company. You must sit in my chair."

"Me? I'm not ready, Mamma."

"But, you are. You have done nothing but succeed, my love. My trust and faith in you have been rewarded beyond my first expectations. You are a diamond. You add sparkle to these old bones. And I am tired, so tired. I need to step down, to look at my life. To disengage."

"Mamma, are you ill?"

Instead of speaking, Isabella pulled out

documents from a large file. They were x-rays and a doctor's report diagnosing the cancer and providing a prognosis. They both spoke of endings. "Yes, I am, child. I am quite near the end. The doctor says maybe six months. The cancer is inoperable and too late to treat. Besides I am too old and too weak to undergo chemotherapy. I don't want any drugs to prolong a life that is only half-livable. I want to spend the rest of my time getting my affairs in order. I want to see you, my successor, installed as chairwoman of Rosso International. I want to see a little of your success as chair before I close my eyes. May God take me then."

Ella's knees wobbled and she flopped into an armchair. She put her head in her lap, and began to cry. The tears came fast, a flood of sorrow at the thought that this loving mother, who had adopted her and made her who she was today, that this great and good soul would soon die.

"No! No! No, Mamma. You can't go! I need you. You are the only one in this world who loves me. What will I do alone? Who will love me?"

"My child, you will survive. You will thrive and

succeed. That is what I have taught you to do. Now, let's plan the announcement of my resignation, your nomination at the next board meeting, and your first steps as chairwoman."

In the nearly six years since Ella had been adopted by Isabella Rosso, the bond between the two women had grown very close, closer than most natural mothers and daughters. They thought alike. They reacted alike to events. They managed people the same way. All of this was almost instinctual with the two. What wasn't, Isabella taught her adopted daughter. Ella was a very quick learner. Rosso Industries had become a multinational corporation. Rosso International issued stock, created a board of directors, and installed an administrative structure with Isabella Rosso as chairwoman.

From its original business interests in carting, construction, importing, and transportation, only importing remained. The construction businesses had been sold off and the corporation invested in business real estate. The transportation part of the portfolio, which had been land vehicles, turned into investment in a fleet of air freighters under the name Rosso Air. The carting business was sold to the Gaetas, who were beginning to value their legitimate assets a great deal more than they had in the past as it became obvious that the newer immigrant gangs were replacing them in the world of crime, mostly because they were willing to be even more ruthless than the Gaeta family. The only part of Rosso Industries that remained and expanded under Rosso International was the importing business. Ella had tripled the olive oil business and added high end Italian wines. Then she began buying clothing factories in Italy, modernizing them by retooling them, but keeping the experienced Italian craftsmen, and exporting both fabric and haute couture to the U.S. But she didn't stop there. She expanded the exports from Italy to Japan and China. The two countries had an unquenchable thirst for first class European clothing. The result of Ella's genius for doing business was moving Rosso from a profitable family-owned company to a modern multinational corporation with offices in New York, San Francisco, Rome, Tokyo and Beijing. This meant she was constantly on the move, often flying from New York to Tokyo and then on to Rome in a few days' time. Sometimes, she woke up in a four star hotel with no idea of where she was until she looked at her phone.

There was a down side, of course, as there is to anything. She had no love life to speak of, no one in her life to share her life with, save for her mother. Her brothers, Gennaro and Gildo, were installed as mid-level managers in San Francisco and Paris, respectively. Surprisingly, both seemed to thrive away from the spotlight that shined on their mother and then their adopted sister. So, there were no family problems these days, but perhaps the prospect of one on the horizon because Johnny was now coming home after five years of living a monk-like existence in Japan. The question in Ella's mind was what would Johnny do? Would he want to be part of the business? Would he want to be with her? Did he still carry a torch? Ella didn't know. She'd need to find out very soon if she was to take over from Isabella as chair of Rosso International. And this wasn't a given. There would be a struggle of some sort ahead, especially with the Japanese member, Malcolm Ozu, whom Ella knew to be opposed to her. The board was multinational: American, English, Italian, French, Chinese and Japanese. They would choose the next chair of the board. Most of them respected Isabella, not least because she was older and experienced. This counted a good deal with the Chinese. The Italian liked Isabella because she could speak to him in his own language. Ella wasn't at that level yet. She probably never would be. The Frenchman, well perhaps the Frenchman, Ella's ally because she was young and beautiful, two qualities the French admired.

No, nothing was for certain. "Maybe, it's best this way," thought Ella. "I'll be the one who controls the outcome because of what I do, not only who I am."

As soon as he arrived, Johnny knew he couldn't live in Brooklyn at the old home on President Street. No one lived there but his mother, who was often bed-ridden and appeared in failing health. Ella had a condominium under the Manhattan Bridge, an area named DUMBO for short. She had paid two million cash for it a few years back. Despite having her own place, she looked in on Isabella every day. That's where Johnny encountered her.

"Johnny! My God!" Ella exclaimed as she walked toward him with open arms.

Johnny smiled at her, and let her hug him, but he did not hug her back.

"No email. No phone calls. Did I do something to hurt you, Johnny? You didn't even embrace me."

Johnny fumbled for an answer. "It's just that...you know I've been living a very different life. I feel guilty now that I didn't let you know where I was in Japan – I was in Nara, by the way. It's just that...that I have become a very different person. Women have not been part of my life since I had that crush on you. And now I see you again, and I don't know how I feel...or even if I feel anything."

"Johnny, we need some time together. I want to let you know what's been going on with our family and our businesses."

"Okay, Ella, but I couldn't be less interested in money and business although I do want to know how you've been, and I see Mamma is sick, so sick. I should have kept in touch."

"We can't go forward if we dwell on our past mistakes. Today is Thursday. I'm booked full until tomorrow evening. How about we spend some time together next weekend? I have a summer home in East Hampton. I'll be in Connecticut next Thursday, and will ferry over, then drive to my place. Meet you there?"

"Fine, but…"

"'Til then. I'm going to spend tonight here with Mamma before I leave. I'll text you the address."

"Text me? I don't own a cell phone."

"Then, I'll write it on the note pad by the downstairs phone before I leave tonight."

119

"Okay, but can I take a train there?"

"The LIRR Montauk line, I'll pick you up at the station."

When Ella left, Johnny went to his old room, shut the lights and closed the door. He needed to meditate on this meeting with his adopted sister. In the darkness, he sat in the middle of the hardwood floor in position for *zazen*. He focused on his breath, in and out. He opened his mind. A phrase came with the breath in, "I want my sister." It repeated over and over. Johnny couldn't let it go, and he hated himself for it. She was his weakness. She was the woman he wanted. He couldn't have her.

CHAPTER ELEVEN
Not Married to the Mob

Jimmy never liked summer all that much. It
reminded him of the heat and stink of the ghetto
streets in Brooklyn, of young punks waiting on
brownstone stoops to challenge each other, of girls
flirting to trap a guy into fatherhood and
responsibility. But up here in Willow, the breeze
brushed the leaves of the trees and the sound was
pleasant. Jimmy liked it. He liked all the greenery. He
marveled at how many trees there were and how thick
the understory grew beneath. If he got really hot, he
headed for the Saw Kill, the Ashokan Reservoir,
Echo Lake, or Cooper Lake. The water was clear and
pure, not like the green gunk and slime of the East

River or the salty beaches of dirty sand at Coney Island and Rockaway.

Life was good. The Gaetas seemed to be moving away from murder, no more ordering hits. Jimmy'd heard they were heading legit. He hoped that was true because he wanted out of his role as a mob hit man even though it would mean no money from the Gaetas. He didn't care. He could live with Star in her place. He already did most every day of the week.

Star had asked him to marry her, and Jimmy said yes. They started to plan the event. Get a priest. Find a church. Invite folks, just none from Jimmy's side. He had no family, no one from the city that he wanted to see, no one he wanted to let know that he was living in Willow. The kids were getting into the spirit of it. Star's daughter, Maisie, began to page through wedding catalogues she borrowed from her friend's mother, hunting for "the perfect dress." She wanted to look pretty and sophisticated for the ceremony. After all she was now a teenager. Davie was dragged into her search, but he was more focused on the fact that he could call Jimmy Dad, something he'd never been able to do with any man.

Over the five plus years that Jimmy'd been upstate, he made maybe ten hits, all of them mob-related. The second one was the only cop he had killed, but that cop had been dirty and tried to double cross the Gaetas. When Jimmy totaled up his plusses and minuses over the years, he came to the conclusion that things were decidedly on the plus side. It was just that the work, which was only once in a long while, was dirty. He knew that. He knew it, so he tried to bury it, tried to focus on his life with Star and her kids.

Jimmy kept up his shooting chops by frequenting local rifle ranges. It was his skill with a rifle that earned him the respect of local hunters and gun enthusiasts when they saw him on the practice range. He gained a reputation as a dead eye shot, and thus invitations came to go hunting with a small group of wealthy locals who invited him along because of his prowess. Around the area, Jimmy was in demand as an instructor, a job he took to despite never having taught anyone anything before. He also had a part

time job at a rod and gun shop off the Thruway.
Jimmy was born Jaime Garcia Diaz but no one
questioned Jimmy Diamond. He had a clean record
because he had a false name, social security card, birth
certificate and driver's license. The Gaetas had seen to
these documents, so that the cops and the feds would
have no way to link the old Jimmy to the new one,
their shooter.

Jimmy's obligation to the Gaeta's was fulfilled
swiftly in no more than a day or so, and not often.
Star never questioned him when he said he had to go
into the city on business, that he would be back in no
more than a day or two. He was always good to his
word. She trusted him, trusted him with the children,
trusted him with her heart. Their impending marriage
was her final step to complete trust and faith in him.

Through the years, the Gaetas had been as good
as their word: they paid him a grand a hit and still
paid for his expenses on the house in Willow, even
though he was hardly there. And through the years,
they had followed a similar pattern: a sudden phone
call to be ready the next day, a car with Gaeta soldiers

to pick him up, a target for the hit given with minimal information and no explanation, a night in a safe house, and a ride back up the Thruway a day later.

A day's notice. That was the problem when the phone call came. Jimmy and Starr were to be married on a sunny and warm day at the tail end of June. Jimmy didn't show up at the rented house in Willow. He was at St. John's Church in Woodstock with Star and the kids. Friends, both his and Star's, were in attendance as well. The reception was to be back at Star's place. Jimmy had received the phone call the night before. He knew that it was useless to ask for a day's delay. The Gaetas required total obedience. They did not negotiate. So, Jimmy just ignored the phone call. After the wedding, on the next morning, Jimmy received a second phone call.

"Congratulations, Jimmy. Too bad your bride might be a widow soon or could it be that you'll be a widower? You fucked up Jimmy, and you gotta pay for it. Bye bye, Jimmy. Bye bye, Star, Bye bye, Maisie. Bye bye Davie."

The call panicked Jimmy. That was its purpose. But he had to think straight. What to do? He couldn't just up and leave with a wife and two kids. The Gaetas would find them no problem. He didn't want to think about what they would do when they did. He had to stay and defend his new family, somehow, some way. He had to make the Gaetas find that it was better to leave him alone than to hunt him down. He had to make the next move.

"Star, I gotta ask ya somethin', and ya gotta do it without knowin' everything."

"Sure, Jimmy. We're man and wife. I'll do whatever you ask of me 'cause I know you love me."

"Good. Here's what I need ya to do. Take the kids and go upstate to your sister's place in Tonawanda, and don't tell no one where you're goin'.

"What'll I tell the kids?"

"Make it a holiday for the kids. It'll be the Fourth of July, okay? Have a good time. When it's time for ya t' come back, I'll call ya. Just give me the number.

Make sure no one knows but your sister."

"What's goin' on Jimmy that you can't tell me?"

"Oh, I will darlin'. One day I promise. But not today. Just please do what I tell ya to."

And so Star piled the kids into her aging Volvo wagon and headed west on the Thruway towards Buffalo.

Meanwhile Jimmy's mind was focused on how to get out of the situation that he got himself into. It wasn't going to be easy, but he had an idea. The Gaetas only respected strength, not weakness, not talking things out, but being top dog through intimidation, superior strength. Jimmy would strike first. He took the train down to the city and rented a cheap hotel room in Queens, a borough that the wise guys of New York paid little attention to. To them it was all Brooklyn and Manhattan, and perhaps a bit of Staten Island. He would get to President Street, but not to use his rifle. He'd get into Crazy Bobby Gaeta's home, leave him a note and a twenty-two cartridge. That would either enrage Crazy Bobby or frighten him. Either possibility was okay with Jimmy.

It was a hot Brooklyn evening in the first week of July. Humidity hung in the air and promised no release with the darkness. There was no one out on the stoop of the Gaeta brownstone. So far, so good, but Jimmy needed to know who was inside the house. He walked around the alley, which served as a common entrance and exit to all the houses on the street. He didn't see any lights on inside. This was the tricky part. He had to take a chance on exposing himself. He opened the back gate to the Gaeta home and threw some pebbles at the door. They were loud enough to draw anyone inside out to have a look. Then he hid himself in the shadows of the alley. He tried to calm himself down, but he was very nervous. So he took several deep breaths. Then he waited. No one came to answer the door. Palming the twenty-two cartridge and the note in his pocket, he walked quickly down the basement steps of the brownstone, and picked the door lock. He left the note and the cartridge on a table, then turned around and quietly walked away, leaving the back door ajar.

The note read: "You taught me good, so good I can get in and out of your house without you knowing it. I can also shoot damn well from a football field away. Think about it. Leave me alone and I do the same. Come for me, and I come for you."

Jimmy hopped a bus to Manhattan and got the train back to Woodstock. Part one of his plan had gone okay. When he got to Woodstock, Jimmy drove his little Chevy Aveo back to the house in Willow. Willy and Big Joey knew his car. He'd bought it off a lot for a good price, complete with snow tires, which he kept on all year round. Willy and Big Joey made fun of his little car. "It's just like you, Jimmy, a little shit," Big Joey jeered.

Willy and Big Joey were lazy. Jimmy was counting on this. He thought they'd come in the light of day, somewhere around ten or eleven in the morning. He intended to be in the forest with a pair of high resolution binoculars.

Sure enough around 10:30 the morning after

Jimmy returned home, Willy parked his Caddy on the road near the house. Then he and Big Joey, guns drawn, split up and started toward the house, Willy walking towards the front, Joey toward the back. Joey got in first through the back door. He checked out each room, but no one was there. He opened the door for Willy. There was a note on the table.

It read: "Hide and seek. Where could I be?"

"Betcha the little prick is in the damned woods," Big Joey said. "You wanna go look?"

"Stupid. He's got a rifle and he can shoot. No way. Let's just make ourselves comfortable here 'til he shows up. If he's out there, he has to come in here or at least through the woods out to the road. We'll get him."

So, the wait began. Jimmy hiked out of the forest preserve, leaving his rifle in a hunting blind he knew of, north of the house. He hiked around the house and out on to the road. He hitched into Woodstock. It was easy to get a ride. Everybody knew him. He spent the afternoon having a good lunch and taking in a film. Just before dark, he headed back to the house, retracing his earlier route away from it. He got his rifle and noiselessly walked towards the north side of the house, which had just a small bathroom window and a skylight ten feet up on the inside wall. He was waiting for Willy or Big Joey to peak outside. He would put a bullet in one of them, not to kill, but to hurt and warn that he could end a man's life in a split second.

Big Joey walked out onto the front porch. He stretched his arms out. "It's cooler out here, Willy. Come on out."

Willy followed, his head swiveling front left to right to scan for Jimmy. Then two pops. Big Joey went down first, and Willy landed on top of him. Big Joey took a bullet in the buttocks. Willy took a bullet in the calf. They scrambled back inside, keeping low. They spent the rest of that night bleeding in pain, fighting sleep, guns in hand, waiting for Jimmy's next move. But there was no move. Jimmy left the area after he shot each of them. He buried the rifle under a pile of leaves just beyond the house property line.

Then he went into town for dinner.

Jimmy returned to the house in the morning after checking to see the Caddy was gone. He'd bought a disposable cell phone at CVS and now he dialed the number Willy had given him years ago. He hadn't used it even once. He was using it now. "Don't come back" is all he said. And they never did.

It wasn't because they were afraid of Jimmy, but Crazy Bobby couldn't afford to lose any more men. Willy and Big Joey were out of commission, nursing their wounds. Gaeta's Mafia family was growing weaker and smaller, and he was feeling the pressure from the black, Latin and Russian gangs. Bobby was focused on making money. Revenge was a luxury. They wrote Jimmy off as a bad investment, but kept the memory alive just in case they came across Jimmy one day at the right place and time.

The day after, Jimmy called Star in Tonawanda. "Hey baby! Time to come home." She got in just after dark. Jimmy was waiting for her at her home. Star didn't ask him about what he had done. Jimmy didn't offer to explain. It was better that way. They just began again from that day, building their family together.

CHAPTER TWELVE:
Disciple

It was late July. The dog days of summer were on
their way. The City was everyone's enemy. Anyone
who could headed for the Jersey shore, Fire Island,
the Hamptons, or some place cool in the Catskills.
Only the poor, the old and the young were left on city
streets. And Johnny.

He still didn't have a clue. He was waiting for
inspiration to come. It would have, if this were Japan.
It wasn't Japan. It was Brooklyn, fuckin' Brooklyn.
What's he going to do? He wished the sen-sei were
here to tell him what to do. "Shit!" he thought. "I
gotta clear my head. Sen-sei sent me here to teach

135

aikido, to spread the message, the practice. But there are so many martial arts studios now: Thai boxing, Korean taekwando, Japanese karate, Brazilian capoeira, Israeli krav maga. They're all over the five boroughs, so how can I attract students? Sen-sei sent me here confident that I was ready. But am I?"

He was on the LIRR out to the Hamptons. Ella was already there. They would talk. Ella mentioned that the sea air and ocean views of her summer home would be just the remedy for his indecision blues.

Passengers who got on the train at Penn Station with Johnny gave him a prolonged once over. They could tell that he wasn't a New Yorker. His clothing. His demeanor. His posture. His gaze. All spoke of another place and time. Johnny felt like a stranger in his own hometown. He was a stranger. He found it hard to relax, to sprawl over empty seats the way everyone seemed to do. He had little in the way of luggage. He didn't own a bathing suit. He was wearing Japanese *jinbei*, a loose fitting top and bottom; the top sleeves not reaching the wrists and the bottom legs falling just below the knees. He had on one of the

Japanese tee shirts the sen-sei had made to promote the dojo in Nara. Johnny's tee had black kanji on an off gray background. "Peace and Health through Aikido" the characters said. To the passengers, the characters merely looked like interesting decorative lines, no message given or received. No one could guess that the kanji were part of a poem done with mastery in the Japanese art of *shodo*. On his feet, Johnny wore rubber beach sandals. He had no hat against the summer sun. All his possessions were stored in a cloth bag suspended from his shoulder: change of underwear, a second tee shirt, razor, toothbrush, and a book of Japanese *manga, Hajime no Ippo*.

At Babylon, a group of gang bangers got on the train. There were five guys all in colors: denim jackets with cut off sleeves and the word *Demons* on a patch across the back. A blonde girl and a brunette girl were with the boys. All of them appeared to be high. After moving about the carriages for a few minutes, the group stumbled upon Johnny. They stopped in front of him. They fixed their gazes on him.

Before the gang bangers came in, Johnny had been reading his manga.

"Hey, bro! Wha's that ya readin'? Some Chink book?" This was the oldest and meanest looking of the group.

Johnny looked up at him. "No, it's Japanese."

"It ain't Japanese. I know 'cause the Japs have their own alphabet, don't they. They ain't use those Chink letters, right?"

"If you're referring to *hirogana* and *katakana*, yes they are Japanese, but the Japanese also used characters that they borrowed from Chinese. They are called kanji."

"You sayin' I'm wrong?"

"No, you're not wrong. There's just a little more to it."

"What are you anyway, some professor?"

"No, just a follower on the path."

"The path of what?"

"Aikido."

"So, you know karate, hunh?"

"No, aikido."

"Lemme see you do somethin'. What if I was to punch you in the face?"

The others laughed at this. They anticipated a little action, a little fun with the lame guy sitting down in the pajamas.

"Hey, why you wearin' pajamas on the train?"

"They're not pajamas. They are Japanese jinbei, casual clothing."

"Everything I say, you gotta contradic' me, ain'tcha?"

Johnny looked at the muscular young man. He saw anger in his eyes. He saw despair. He saw a soul with no release. "Is there some way I can help you?" he asked.

"Yeah, you can get up and give your seat to my lady here." And with that he grabbed the blonde, who wore a halter top with no bra, and short shorts with sandals. Most of her body was on display.

"Easy, Magic Man. You gonna make my boobs pop outta my top."

Magic Man put his arm around the girl and squeezed her breast as he stuck his tongue in her mouth. Her role was to comply, to act like she loved it.

"Well, let's get with it, bro. A seat for the lady."

"There's one right over there with no one in it."

"You tellin' me where my lady gotta sit. Stand up bro'. I'm gonna teach you a lesson."

Magic Man cocked his right fist and flexed once or twice for his gang, popping his biceps up and down. He smiled. They laughed. Then he turned to Johnny with anger in his eyes. He stepped forward to hit Johnny in the jaw.

It was like that time years ago: Johnny saw sensei bring down the bozo steroid user at the twenty-four hour gym. This time he was the sen-sei. Johnny evaded the punch, swung himself under the boy's huge arm, grabbing it for leverage. He brought him down as he did so with a short quick movement of his hands. Magic Man crumpled to the floor.

Two more of the gang came at Johnny, one with a knife, the other with a bicycle chain. In no more than the blink of an eye, each attacker was subdued, and his weapon removed. The remaining gang bangers just stood in shock that this weird guy, who looked like he was meat for their rough games, could so easily floor three of them in seconds.

Magic Man was trying hard to catch his breath. The blow was to his ego as well as his body. It had taken his breath away. "What are youse?" he barely breathed out the question.

"I am a teacher of aikido," Johnny replied. And for the first time, he believed it. So, he said it again. "I am a teacher of aikido."

Magic Man looked at him.

"Would you like to learn?" Johnny asked. "Give me your phone number. When I set up my dojo, I will call you. What is your name?"

"Marvin Reichman, but my friends call me Magic Man."

"And why is that?" Johnny asked.

"Because until today, my hands been magic. I never lost a fight."

Johnny extended his right hand to Marvin Reichman, and helped him to his feet. "I'm getting off next stop. Perhaps we'll meet again if you can eat bitter."

"What does that mean?"

"If you come to train with me, you will know." Johnny smiled at Marvin Reichman and the rest of his gang. "Oh, and young lady," Johnny said, turning to the blond girl, "A woman does not give herself away. It is always better to suggest than to show if you know what I mean."

CHAPTER THIRTEEN:
Family Man

Jimmy Diaz had become Jimmy Diamond. No one knew other than the Gaetas, and no one cared other than the Gaetas. They would just as soon have Jimmy dead if he had any importance to them other than, in their view, being an ungrateful mook. However, something was eating at Jimmy, something that was putting his identity to question. He had always told himself he couldn't afford a conscience, but he seemed to be growing one because he was uneasy in his relationship with Star. One day in late fall of their fourth year together, Jimmy sat down with Star for the talk. The kids were asleep. Nothing was on the tube that they cared to watch. Star was leafing through the local paper looking for a used bike for Davie. Star didn't believe in buying something new if something used could do the job just as well. Jimmy liked that about her. She was a woman who knew how to economize and find a bargain, but she wasn't cheap. Quite the opposite, she was generous to her friends and with Jimmy and the kids.

Jimmy opened a Stella. "Star? There's something I gotta tell ya."

"Yeah, baby? What is it?"

"You know how I told you I came up here to get away from the craziness of the city? Well, that's part of the story, but not the main part. I feel like I gotta tell ya everything, so we really know each other."

"Jimmy, I know I love you, and I believe you love me. For me, that's what I really need to know. There're parts of people's lives that they keep to themselves, and for good reason. There're things in my life I don't like to think about."

"Hold on! I gotta speak before I get afraid to. My

real name is Jimmy Diaz. I used to be a street punk and a pimp. I eventually became a hit man for the Mob. They set me up here in Woodstock and called my number when they wanted somebody taken out. They put me in a house, the one up the road in Willow, gave me an allowance, then a thousand bucks when I made the hit. Until our marriage, I was still working for them. I decided to split from them because…because of you and the kids. Believe me they will never touch you. You'll never be in danger."

Starr dropped the paper and looked across the room at her Jimmy, Jimmy Diamond, not Jimmy Diaz. "So that's what that trip to my sister's was all about. That's what those overnights in the city were, your hits, your killing. Jimmy? Jimmy? Tell me."

"Yes, that's what all that was. I had to lie to you then, but see, I can't any longer. I can't hold it inside. I am a different guy, and you are the reason that's so. I love you and the kids. I love our life together. I love working like an ordinary Joe. I only hope my honesty don't push you away from me."

Jimmy's face went soft and he suddenly looked like a dog waiting for a scolding. He hung his head, but his eyes looked up, searching Star's. Star curled her legs under her and pushed herself erect. She held her neck and head ramrod straight and stared at Jimmy. "Do I know you Jimmy? Do I know you as a man who could kill in cold blood? And, if, as you say, that's who you are, were, what do I do now?"

"I guess that's up to you, Star. But I want you to know that you, Maisie and Davie mean the world to me. I am a changed man. I am finally a man, not a street punk, not a killer…"

"But you were a pimp? You sold women?"

"To my shame, I did."

"How could you?"

"I ask myself that, but back then, it was all I could do with who I was. When I grew up, I was alone. My auntie took me in when my father left us and my mom died of an overdose of rock cocaine on the street in front of our apartment. Auntie Clara fed me out of duty, but she didn't love me. My cousins just felt I got in their way, and took the little from them that they couldn't afford to give: one less mouthful of food, one less present at Christmas, one less hour of precious time with their mother, my auntie, who worked three minimum wage jobs on diabetic legs. She was exhausted every night and every morning. On my sixteenth birthday, she died of that exhaustion, and her shitty, joyless life in the Puerto Rican ghetto. Two of my three cousins had reached eighteen. They kept the apartment, but threw me out on the street. I had to figure out how to keep myself alive. I lived on the street. I slept in parks, alleys, and shelters. I begged for spare change. I tried every hustle I could manage. I wound up pimping women, and I moved on to worse, like I just told you."

And with that, Jimmy came to Star and got to his knees.

"I beg you, Star, stay with me. I am so sorry for who I was, but I could only be sorry because of the good you've brought out of me."

Star didn't speak. Instead she cradled Jimmy's head in her lap. Like a priest in the confessionals Jimmy frequented as a child, she forgave him with her own absolution. That night they made love, soft, slow and with their hearts open to each other.

Jimmy went to work at the gun shop, gave shooting lessons, and became a decent cook, continuing his habit of reading recipes, buying ingredients and trying them out on the family. He spent as much time as he could with the kids. He was good with them. He made them laugh. He made them happy. They trusted him. They loved him as a father.

Maisie was fascinated by fashion; she carried around a sketch pad to draw her ideas. At her middle school, she was known for her individualistic fashion sense. She didn't follow the crowd. She led it. Davie was a budding athlete. He was small, but stringy strong, fast as a rabbit with reflexes to match. He was a runner and he raced go-karts. He and Jimmy spent hours tinkering with his go-kart to make it faster.

Things went well for a good long while. Star was

making a name for herself as a quilter. She had frequent local shows. One day she was asked to submit for a show in Brooklyn.

The train conversation resulted in changes for Marvin Reichman and Johnny Rosso. Johnny asked Ella if he could use her large house on Meadow Lane in Southampton as his dojo. He would live in the mother-in-law cottage in back of the main house. His live-in students would have their rooms on the second floor of the main house. The first floor would be for business, for welcoming guests, and it would house the kitchen/dining room. The basement would be the actual aikido training area.

"I had an epiphany of sorts on the train coming out, Ella," Johnny switched between calling his adopted sister Ella, as she was once, and Isabella, as she is now. "I realize that I am an aikido teacher and that I need to start right away. In fact, I found my first student on that train, a young man who tried to assault me."

"You want your first student to be some street tough?"

"Yes, he is perfect for it. He has seen what aikido can do."

"But this house, Johnny. It's right at the end of what they call "Billionaire's Lane" out here. I am not sure that these people would take kindly to having some sort of commercial enterprise near their homes. God, I had a hard enough time buying this place. I was too nouveau riche for most of them. Besides there was only one wealthy person among them whose name ended in a vowel like ours."

"Still," Johnny looked at her.

"Still, you want it. Okay, I get it. I don't really understand how you think, but I can understand that this is important to you. Ella dug into her purse. "Here they are," and she handed the keys over to Johnny. "It's yours for now. It's the least I can do for you. You're the one who started me on the path I now walk. Without you, I wouldn't be Isabella Rosso. Oh, and I'm guessing you have no money. I will help you for a year financially, and then we'll see what's what. Okay?"

"Okay. Thank you, Ella."

"I hope it works, Johnny."

"I do, too," he answered, smiling at his sister.

Marvin Reichman proved to be an ideal student, not least of all because he needed someone to care about him. He gave Johnny his loyalty, his sweat equity, and finally, his filial love. He addressed Johnny as "sen-sei." Over several months, Marvin transformed from an over-muscled loudmouth troublemaker to a lithe, humble student of aikido. Marvin was intelligent and he read voraciously: books on aikido, on Japanese history, Japanese culture, Eastern philosophy, and religion. Johnny enrolled him in an intensive Japanese course at Suffolk Community College in Riverhead. He bought Marvin a used road bike so he could commute from the dojo to the college.

Marvin and Johnny did as many public demonstrations of aikido as they could to attract new students. Within a year, the dojo was full and there were four serious students living in the house on Meadow Lane. Johnny began to train the local police in disarming techniques and how to treat aggressive behavior. This bought him the support of the department and kept the billionaires quiet about the martial arts dojo on "their" lane.

For Johnny, life was right. He was doing what he needed to honor his teacher and himself. Then one day he went to visit his mother's grave. His years in Japan had inculcated in him a profound respect for those in his family who'd gone to their rest. Foremost among these was his mother. On a brisk late fall afternoon, Johnny cleared his mother's grave of old flowers and the detritus that blew across the rows of gravestones in Green-Wood Cemetery. At his side, was his adoptive sister, Ella or Isabella. They met on the anniversary of their mother's death to pray at her grave site, bring fresh flowers, and then share a quiet dinner together. This evening they were heading to

Ciacci's off Court Street. They had an hour to kill before their dinner reservations at seven. Ella suggested they drop in on a nearby gallery that had an exhibit of American quilts.

"I didn't know you were interested in something as old-fashioned as quilts."

"Actually, I am interested, but I have to confess I have more than a passing interest in this art gallery. I am a silent partner. Gina Wills is the gallery director and curator. She's my partner. People think she owns the place, and that's the way I want it. I like to follow my interests without a lot of publicity. At this point, nearly everything I do seems to be worth some reporter's interest. It's the part of being a successful businesswoman that I could do without."

"And the gallery? Where is it?"

Just a block from Ciacci's. It's the GW Gallery. GW for Gina Wills."

"Is that the whole story, Isabella?"

"Well, it is opening night, and I should really

put in an appearance…to support Gina and the gallery, you know."

Johnny and Isabella walked from the now chilly October evening into a hotbox of people, jammed into one large open room. Isabella went looking for Gina while Johnny began to look at the quilts hung around the four walls of the room. A few inches below bottom left of each quilt was the artist's name with a short biography and a statement about the work from the artist.

CHAPTER FOURTEEN:
Mise en Scene

Jimmy, Star, Maisie and Davie drove down to Brooklyn. Star's talent as a quilter got her into an Americana exhibit at the GW Gallery. They were moving around the gallery floor, meeting guests and other artists, as Johnny made his tour of the gallery.

"Star Diamond," he mused under his breath, "Now how does someone get a name like that?"

He must have been speaking loud enough for someone to hear because over his shoulder, a woman said, "I guess it is odd, now that you say it. But it's my name, really and truly. The Star I was given at birth. The Diamond I added with my second marriage," she said, pointing to her husband, who was standing a few feet in back of her, holding hands with two young teens, a boy and a girl.

Johnny looked at the man. Then he looked again. It clicked. The memory of a long ago incident in Brooklyn, a gun shot, Ella kidnapped. "This is the guy who pulled the trigger!" So as not to give himself away, he turned from the man, and engaged the woman in conversation.

"I like the piece a lot."

"It's a portrait of the four of us, outside our home near Woodstock. There's Jimmy playing with Maisie and Davie in the winter snow. There's me looking out the living room window at them. You could say it's my ideal, my vision of how life should be, what a family is…"

Johnny couldn't help himself. "Been married long? You mentioned it was your second."

"Four and a half years now. Five this coming July. I'm a happy woman. First time didn't work.

158

Second time's a charm."

Johnny smiled at her and at the children, who had now come closer to share in their mother's accomplishment. "That's me," said Maisie, "the girl with the rosy cheeks and Cat in the Hat hat. Cool, isn't it?"

"And this guy rolling a giant snowball must be Davie. Am I right?" Johnny asked, looking at the boy.

"Yes sir, That's me. Jimmy, I mean Dad and I are startin' to build a snowman."

"Must have been fun."

"Yeah, it was," Jimmy replied, giving no sign that he had recognized Johnny.

"Well, nice to meet you all," Johnny said by way of leave taking. "I guess I'll make my way around the room."

Johnny's feelings, which had been on such an even keel since his immersion in aikido, tumbled over each other. A deep, growing sense of alarm began to seize him. He felt disoriented, captive of another time and place. He started to practice deep breathing to clear his mind, but it wouldn't work. He moved from quilt to quilt, preoccupied by a sense of danger. After moving through half of the exhibit, he spotted his sister in conversation with a short, pert looking woman, whose wiry rust brown hair sprung in all directions at once, and whose body language radiated perpetual motion.

"Johnny. This is Gina Wills, the gallery curator and director. Gina, my brother Johnny Rosso."

"Pleased to meet you Johnny," Gina grinned at him, eyes wide and blue, hand extended.

"Likewise, Gina."

"Isabella tells me you're quite different from her; you're an aikido teacher, a student of Japanese culture and history, and also monk-like, an ascetic of sorts. Is that right?"

"I don't think of myself as anything more than a simple person, trying to live a life of peace and harmony with others. If that makes me a monk, then so be it." Johnny smiled back at Gina. "You know I do enjoy the occasional beer, a good meal, and the talents of artists. Come to think of it, many monks in the older eastern and western traditions were known to be similar in character that way."

"Well, let me show you around the gallery. That is, with your permission, of course."

"I'd like nothing more," Johnny replied. Momentarily, his sense of impending danger was erased by the woman taking his arm.

"I'll see you at the end of the exhibit," Isabella said as she went off to chat with one of the local quilters. But she didn't get to her because she saw Jimmy, and recognized him right away. She wondered how in the world he was at the gallery. Then she noticed he was with one of the quilters, and that there were two children accompanying them. They were moving toward her, so she chose to move away from them toward the entrance. There she met Crazy Bobby Gaeta along with two of his henchmen, Willy

Arrigo and Joey Taglio. Isabella knew them because each walked with a distinctive limp; Willy kind of hopped, and Joey raised one leg cautiously and slowly before putting it down, so it seemed it took him forever to get anywhere. She knew Crazy Bobby as the head of the Gaeta family. His sisters, Anna and Brigida, and younger brother, Onofrio, had come to her often for business advice. They had their heads in the new century while Crazy Bobby seemed to think that Italian Mafiosi still ruled the streets of New York. Crazy Bobby got his nickname because he would do anything on a dare. When he was a kid, his cousin Vinny dared him to stick a pencil in his eye for five dollars. Bobby did. As a result, he earned his nickname and a trip to the hospital, where surgeons saved his right eye but not the sight in it. Bobby's right eye seemed to roll around in its socket, thereby reinforcing the idea of his craziness. He was a solid block of a man with dirty blond hair that he chose to wear in a nineteen-fifties style with sides swept to a DA in back and the top buzzed short. He favored flashy suits and lots of rings on his fingers. There was always a visible bulge behind his lapel pocket where he kept a forty-five loaded and ready.

"Donna Rosso, Com'e' bella!" Bobby exclaimed, using the old Sicilian honorific.

"Just Ms. Rosso will do Mr. Gaeta, and thank you for the compliment. You're looking well today yourself. I had no idea you were interested in art. It's the first time I've seen you in this gallery."

"Well, there's a first time for everything, Ms. Rosso," Bobby replied, drawing out the sibilant of Ms. as if to mock Isabella.

"Your brother and sisters must have had some influence on you after all Mr. Gaeta. They've perhaps moved you out of the last century." Isabella knew how to handle herself in conversation, and she did not fear Gaeta.

"Hey, you don't know me, Ms. Rosso. I'm a modern guy. Now, if you'll excuse me, me and the boys will look at this art." Gaeta, Arrigo and Taglio moved into the crowded room, Gaeta leading, his two crippled henchmen following behind. Gaeta was looking for Jimmy, and he found him and the children near Star's quilt.

"I got eyes and ears everywhere, Jimmy. You knew you wouldn't see the last of me, you fuckin' prick. Let's move out of here nice and slow. Willy and Joey got something they wanna settle wit' you. Me too, for that matter."

Arrigo grabbed Maisie's hand, and Taglio put his thick arm on Davie's shoulder. The kids didn't know what to do, so they followed their dad who was arm and arm with Gaeta, heading towards the gallery door. Star hadn't seen what happened. She was deep in conversation with a fellow quilter on the opposite side of the gallery. The only one who noticed what was going on was Johnny, who had just about concluded a trip around the gallery, escorted by Gina Wills. "Gina, I need to go outside for just a minute. I'll be right back, I promise."

"Sure, Johnny," Gina smiled at him. Something had clicked for Gina. She couldn't wait for Johnny to rejoin her. "Can I go out with you? I could use a little fresh air, Johnny."

"I'll be right back, Gina. No need for you to go out in this cold. I think it's starting to rain, too. Better stay dry."

"Sure, Johnny, but come right back. There's some more I'd like you to see."

Johnny followed the Gaetas, Jimmy and the children. He saw them walk into an alleyway about half a block north of the gallery. Instead of confronting them – he knew something was wrong when he saw the Gaeta henchmen grab the children – he watched from the corner of the alley. He saw Arrigo pull out a gun and point it at Jimmy. The children began to cry. Taglio's big hands covered both their mouths and faces to keep them quiet. Gaeta began to pummel Jimmy, who knew better than to resist. His only hope was that a beating would be the end of it. On the cold ground of the dirty alleyway, Jimmy absorbed blow after blow. Gaeta's anger grew with each punch and kick he delivered. Jimmy's face was bloody. Then Maisie bit Taglio's hand, and ran for the street. Arrigo turned his gun on her, and shot once. The child fell.

"Asshole, why did ya shoot the kid? It's the Spic we wanted. Now we gotta get the fuck outta here and quick. No more shootin'. Cabeesh?" Gaeta and his men ran toward the street, not pausing to look at Maisie. That's when Johnny struck. He tripped Gaeta, who went face first into the cement sidewalk. Then he disarmed Arrigo and pointed the gun at him and Taglio.

"I've never shot a man, but then I've never seen a man shoot a child. Put your hands on the wall and spread your legs out," he ordered the henchmen. Meanwhile Jimmy crawled towards Maisie, who was bleeding profusely into the cold dirty surface of the alley.

"Hold this the gun while I check the girl," Johnny ordered.

Jimmy grabbed the gun, but he didn't just hold it. Beaten and weakened as he was, he still had a true aim. He shot each man in rapid succession: Gaeta first, then Arrigo, then Taglio. Gaeta in both hands, Arrigo in his good leg, and Taglio in the buttocks again.

"Bastards!" he cried out. Then he collapsed.

Johnny created a makeshift bandage from the sweater he was wearing, and tied it gently round Maisie's stomach, but tight enough to absorb the blood from her wound. Davie clung to his sister's legs.

The noise of the gunshots had drawn visitors out of the gallery. Police were soon on the scene. An ambulance followed and took all six individuals to Long Island Cottage.

Chapter Fifteen:
Police Work

Detective Buddy Murphy was at his wits end. He had spent the last two days in the hospital questioning Jimmy, Gaeta, Arrigo and Taglio. His partner, Detective Gerry Casserly, interrogated Johnny and Davie. Maisie was in intensive care with Star at her bedside day and night. All Murphy could get out of anyone was that no one knew who shot them. They didn't recognize anyone. It was too dark. Jimmy claimed that he had been the victim of a mugging, coincidentally, and found himself in the alleyway near the three men with bullet wounds. Each of them denied knowing who Jimmy was. No one knew why Maisie was shot.

Detective Casserly, didn't hear much of anything from Johnny and Davie. Johnny told some of the truth. He had gone outside. He did follow the children, but he only went into the alley after he heard a gunshot. He didn't see a gun because he went straight to help the bleeding child. Johnny didn't know the Gaetas, but he did recognize Jimmy. He told Casserly that he thought he knew Jimmy from his days as a social worker in the Brooklyn ghetto. He said nothing about Jimmy shooting him and kidnapping Ella. Davie told Casserly what he remembered before Taglio covered his face: that the men took him, his sister and Jimmy out of the gallery. Davie didn't know who shot his sister. He said Taglio had his big hand over his mouth and eyes when it happened.

Murphy and Casserly tried to piece together the stories they were getting from the men and the boy. There was no weapon. Isabella, her wits about her, had run out of the gallery and, taking in the scene in the alley, grabbed the gun from Jimmy's hand before anyone could notice. She hid it in the gallery. No one had seen her do it save for Gina.

The detectives knew Gaeta and his henchmen as part of a larger old Mafia family. In recent years, they'd been reduced in size and activity, mostly quiet, not active in the gangland killings that still plagued New York City. They were considered minor players now, not like the Russians, the Colombians, and other newer immigrant gangs. Still there had to be a way that all this made sense for the Gaetas and for Jimmy Diamond, whom they had identified through prints as a once small time pimp and gangbanger formerly known as Jimmy Diaz. Where was the weapon? Why was Jimmy beaten to a pulp? Who shot the Gaetas? Who shot the little girl and why? None of it seemed to make sense. Then there's this other guy, a former New York City social worker, now an aikido instructor from the Hamptons. What was he doing in Brooklyn? What were they all doing near the art gallery? A difficult puzzle indeed with no information forthcoming from the shooting victims and an odd story from the aikido instructor and the boy. The little girl was in intensive care for quite a while. Though she was nearly out of critical condition, she was still sedated and under twenty-four hour watch, her mother sleeping in a cot next to her.

No matter how they tried, Murphy and Casserly couldn't get the Gaetas to change their stories. Jimmy stuck to his as well. Maisie finally recovered enough to be discharged from the hospital, but she didn't speak. Doctors said it was some sort of delayed reaction to the trauma she'd been through. Star insisted that the family be allowed to go home to Woodstock. Jimmy was in awful shape and could hardly move. Davie was very worried about his stepfather, Jimmy, and just wanted to forget the whole awful nightmare he'd witnessed. Jimmy needed to stay in the hospital longer for fear of internal bleeding. The Brooklyn detectives allowed the rest of the family to return after securing the cooperation of the local police to put a round the clock watch on their home. Johnny was released the same night as the incident with the proviso that he return to Brooklyn should he be wanted for further questioning. Weeks went by. No new evidence turned up. No new witness came forward. Murphy and Casserly had a growing caseload and couldn't afford to linger over what happened near the art gallery that night. The only one who got a decent answer was Gina Wills. She met Isabella for an espresso the next day. The two sat and talked about the incident.

"So what happened Isabella?"

"Your guess is as good as mine."

"Oh come on. It's me. I saw you take the gun and hide it in the office."

"Okay, Gina. The things I'm going to tell you might shock you a bit, so sit tight. Don't interrupt, and listen with an open mind."

"Shoot," answered Gina.

"Poor choice of words, kiddo," smiled Ella. Then she briefly sketched her personal history, her relationship to Jimmy and to Johnny, and her dealings with the Gaetas. Gina sat through it all, her eyes growing wider at each turn of the story.

"You were a runaway junkie? I can't believe it!"

"It's true, Gina. I'm a walking example that determination and good luck can change a life. Bad timing can ruin a life, too. And this incident couldn't have been timed worse. Thank God the outcome wasn't fatal for any of them. I wince each time I think of those kids being brutalized by the Gaeta mobsters. I also say a prayer for Maisie, who's still traumatized, and for Jimmy and his new family."

"Despite all he put you through?"

"Yes, and thank God for Johnny. He stopped things from getting worse. I wish Jimmy didn't shoot those thugs, but I can certainly understand why he did."

"Wow! The whole thing takes my breath away."

"Let's put it behind us, Gina. This gallery is for art and art can heal even the darkest of souls. Let's work toward that end."

The whole thing got under Buddy Murphy's skin. In twenty-three years on the force, most of them spent dealing with Mafiosi and the new immigrant gangs, this was the strangest damn thing he'd ever come across. It began to preoccupy him to the exclusion of everything else. It entered into his mind when he rose early for daily mass. It followed him to work. He couldn't rest, couldn't feel right, until he made sense of it all. Three Mafiosi shot, but not killed. One Puerto Rican street trash beaten badly, different now, but still a former pimp and God knew what else, in a hospital room near the three, connected to them somehow. Somebody cracked his ribs and nearly crushed his spleen. Somebody made his face look like a pin cushion.

Murphy wondered whether the boy, Davie, was telling the truth, and why the little girl was one of the shooting victims in the sad affair. The weirdo martial arts guy, Johnny, was brother to Isabella Rosso, queen of a business empire. The two of them couldn't be more different. And then, too, the Rossos were once active Mafiosi, but no more. The Gaetas were still in the game. How did they figure together? Why were they all in the same damn place at the same time? Buddy had to find out, so he could get it all straight and out of his head. If that meant some digging and putting off more active cases, so be it. Casserly was a good partner. Buddy, an old-school guy, didn't even mind that his partner was a woman, and married with kids to boot. Gerry'd be in on it with him.

His first break came when he remembered looking at Bobby Gaeta's hands as they brought him into the hospital. His hands were swollen and his knuckles were raw. First, Murphy paid it no mind. After all, Gaeta'd been shot through each palm. Natural for the hand to swell. But Gaeta's hands looked like he'd just worked someone over. Bingo! He'd beat the Puerto Rican to a pulp! Murphy interrogated both of them again, but their stories never changed. However, there was something else. The Puerto Rican's prints were on file and Murphy'd had the presence of mind to get a fresh set after they settled Diaz in his hospital bed. They matched. Then he thought about what that meant for Diaz and

Gaeta. Nothing, until what Casserly found out.

"Buddy, I got Diaz's prints. He's done time. He's been out of circulation for ages. Changed his name to Diamond. Married. Lives near Woodstock. And maybe he had a strong tie to the Gaetas. There was some buzz years ago that Crazy Bobby had farmed out his hits."

"Gaeta farmed out his hits! Shit! That's gotta mean something here. Have we got any unsolved with prints?"

"No, but I can check. I'll call you if I find anything in the open cases."

Not an hour later, Casserly called to tell Murphy that Diaz's prints matched a set recovered from Arnold Goldman's doorbell. The accountant to the mob's murder had remained unsolved.

"Bingo! Gotcha Spic!" Murphy said to himself.

But he really had nothing. No gun. No witness. Diaz was Diamond living in fucking Woodstock when Goldman got hit. He asked Casserly to talk to

Goldman's widow. She'd remarried and lived with her new husband on the upper West Side, quite a step up from her Queens row-house. She dressed well. It looked like she had money. She gave Casserly nothing when she interviewed her. All sadness and concern about the murder of her "Dear Arnie," but claiming not to know a thing about Goldman's work for the mob.

Murphy drove up to Woodstock to interview Star and the kids. Daisie still wasn't talking though she was a lot better. The bullet had pierced her right lung and she got out of breath when she ran, but she was physically better. She just didn't talk. Davie turned out to know very little because the "big man," as he called Taglio, had covered his eyes during the action. Star was adamant in her defense of her husband. She said he had occasional business in the city, but that he was ninety-nine percent of the time with the family in Woodstock. She said Jimmy was a good man. She thought she knew about his past because he had told her about it. He was honest with her, and he loved her and the kids. Star didn't understand why the detective wanted to bother them. It was bad enough that Jimmy was mugged and seriously hurt.

Murphy was going nuts. He could feel he was close to something big. He could feel that Jimmy was involved with the Gaetas, that something went wrong between them, that Jimmy was given a beating close to death for it. But damn it! What was it? Nobody talked. Not Jimmy. Not the Gaetas. He even took the train out to Southampton to talk to Johnny Rosso. It was like talking to a Sphinx, one riddle after another, spoken in truth, but impenetrable. Rosso told him about the visit to his mother's grave with his sister, their dinner together, and the visit to the art gallery that she owned. That all made sense, but nothing else did. Murphy spoke to Isabella Rosso. She only said that she saw the men on the ground, and called 911 on her cell.

Murphy finally realized he had to let the whole thing go or suffer the consequences of neglecting his case load, which grew bigger every week. There was no shortage of gang activity: the Crips, the Bloods, the Latin Kings, the Trinitarios, the New Dons, MS-13, the Russian mafia, the Albanian mafia, the Serbian mafia. "It was simpler when it was just the Guineas," he thought to himself as he buried the file on Jimmy Diaz.

Johnny returned to Brooklyn to see Isabella a few weeks after the incident. He felt that he had to get himself straightened out before he could teach again. Marvin was far enough along to do the work of the dojo while he was away. One evening he and Isabella were having dinner at her condo.

"Isabella, you had the presence of mind to get rid of the gun. But I wonder why. What made you do just that?"

"I'd recognized Jimmy, and of course, I know Bobby Gaeta and his men. My first impulse was to call 911, but I didn't until I got the gun. Then I called. I saw you weren't hurt and that you were attending to the little girl. I figured the next thing was to dispose of evidence. I had no idea who shot the girl. I knew it

180

couldn't be you, but I didn't know who it was. Jimmy as the shooter didn't make sense either. I saw him with the children and with Star Diamond, the quilter whose work is hanging in the exhibit. I didn't know what to do other than to get that gun away from the bodies lying on the ground."

"Did I ever tell you about the redhead?"

"The redhead?"

"Yeah, I used to have these dreams where I was in danger and the redhead was there, sometimes to save me, yet the dreams always left me with a sense of foreboding. I haven't had one for a long time, not since before I left for Japan."

Johnny hesitated and cast his eyes downward as if looking into his own soul. "I had one of those dreams on the day of the opening. I wouldn't have told you about it, but with what's happened, it's like the dreams are premonitions of evil."

"Johnny, you can't believe that."

"But I do. And now the dream's return coupled

with the events outside the gallery that night have got me frightened once again. Once again, I feel rudderless and anxious."

CHAPTER SIXTEEN:
A Reminder

Jimmy got back to Woodstock the day before Thanksgiving. He hadn't heard much from Star since the incident. He figured she was preoccupied with Maisie. Star didn't know he was coming. When she heard the taxi door slam, and saw Jimmy gingerly walking towards her with a small bag in one hand and flowers in the other, her heart melted.

"For you," he said, moving to embrace her.

Star looked up into his eyes. "Jimmy, what happened to us? You, Maisie, those men. I couldn't even get in to see you. You were hurt so bad. The police had an officer posted outside your door;

wouldn't let anyone in, including me."

"Remember my story? Those were the ones who controlled me, Bobby Gaeta and his men. They were looking for payback because I wouldn't work for them no more. I am so sorry about Maisie; they used the kids to make sure I wouldn't do anything. Willy shot Maisie. I don't even know why, some kind of instinct to shoot at a moving target, someone's back."

"My daughter! You put her and Davie in danger."

"Our daughter. Our kids. I know and I hate myself for that, but it's all in the past."

"What will happen next?"

"Next? There is no next. It's over."

"You said that before."

"This time it's true. They can't move against me. The cops are watching the Gaetas' every move. My every move, too. But I'm here with you and the kids. I'm no gangster."

They went into the house. Davie was watching a movie on Netflix, and barely registered that Jimmy was back. Maisie sat in an armchair, lost in a fashion magazine. When she saw Jimmy, her eyes got wide. Her expression was first that of a frightened child, but a smile broke through.

"Maisie, darling. How are you? How's my girl?"

With her eyes, Maisie said okay, but no sound passed her lips.

"What's going on?" Jimmy asked as he drew near Star.

In a whispered voice, she replied, "Maisie hasn't said a word since the shooting. She's fine physically, but the trauma she went through has scarred her psychologically. Her therapist says it's a matter of time until she finds she can speak. Right now, not speaking keeps the horror she went through away from her. If she doesn't talk about it, no one else can really. She needs to speak and to speak about her shooting."

"What about school?"

"I've been collecting her assignments and textbooks. I work with her here at home."

"But how does she communicate with you? How do you know she understands, that her brain ain't damaged?"

"We use gestures, touch, facial expressions, she writes, and most of all, she speaks with her eyes."

And so the days passed. Jimmy went back to work. Davie went to school. Star worked with the silent Maisie at home. One day a post card came with the ordinary paper spam of advertisements and charity requests for donations. It was a peculiar, almost sacrilegious sort of card. There was a man naked from the waste spread-eagled on a wooden cross. His arms were tied with rope, and where the nails were on Christ's hands, there were what looked like bullet holes. The man appeared to be in his sixties. He had blond hair, going gray but styled in a youngish kind of way from another era. His head hung down on his chest. His left eye was closed, but his right one was half open and staring out of the photo at the viewer. On the back of the card was a single sentence, "I will rise again." Davie was the first one to see it and he showed it to Jimmy.

"Dad, what's this?" Davie asked.

Jimmy's eyes grew wide, and a momentary expression of alarm swept over his face. Then he pulled himself together. "Just some nut trying to get a rise out of people. I wonder how many others got the same postcard?"

The postcard was a message from Crazy Bobby that things weren't over yet. Jimmy didn't know how and when, but the Gaetas were coming after him. He made sure that Star didn't see the postcard although Davie told her about the weird postcard with a guy pretending to be Jesus Christ. When she asked, Jimmy told Star he had thrown it away. But he hadn't. He put it in his gun locker at the house in Willow.

CHAPTER SEVENTEEN:
Worry

Training a gun on a human being was against every principle that Kobayashi Sen-Sei had taught him. Johnny felt unhinged by the incident outside the GW Gallery. He kept turning it over in his mind, trying to find a way back to the path of right living, but how could he when all he could visualize was a gun in his hand? That was not the way of aikido. Johnny began to doubt that he even understood the way, to doubt that he was worthy of the way. What right did he have to teach? What claim did he have to non-violent living? He kept vacillating in his mind from aikido teacher to rudderless human being.

He was safer and saner in the routines of his dojo in Southampton; there he hid from his memory, or at least he tried to. Still, he felt himself defeated by the events of the recent past. On a rainy windy morning as he walked along the seashore in Southampton, he saw a dory come unmoored. "That's like my belief. It's drifting away from me." He began to sing in a whisper a snippet of a Christian hymn he once knew. 'You're drifting too far from the shore.' "It fits, fits me to a tee," he thought.

Isabella was worried. First of all, she was worried about Johnny. She'd thought that he had found himself as an aikido teacher. He seemed secure, content. But since the incident, he was again the uncertain, unfocused Johnny. She hated to see him that way. It made her feel inadequate too, like she couldn't take care of those she cared for despite all her accomplishments as a business woman.

Her relationship with Gina was becoming strained over the gun. "Where is the gun now,

Isabella? Is it still here in the gallery? I don't want it here. Please, get rid of it. You shouldn't have taken it in the first place. You're not," Gina hesitated. "You're not a criminal, so why keep the gun?" The third point of concern for her was the Gaeta family, particularly Crazy Bobby. He had created the scene in her gallery for a reason, but she didn't know what it was. Perhaps he wanted to provoke her, show her she was no better than him.

Then there was Jimmy. Years had passed since she'd thought of him at all, but there he was again. He seemed changed. She hoped that was the case. But he was involved with the Gaetas, and that could come to no good.

Last of all, there were those two detectives. They weren't satisfied with the statements they'd taken. Things didn't make sense to them. She could see that. They barely made sense to her. It was a blessing that Murphy and Casserly had stopped bugging her lately. She didn't know how much more she could take of their suspicions and their repetition of the same questions, looking for inconsistencies in her answers.

It rattled her.

For Jimmy Diamond, life had been kind these last years. But the past didn't let him go. Jimmy had mostly forgotten about the work he had done for the Gaetas. There was one thing he couldn't forget. He was a cop killer. He killed Michael Maher and left his wife a widow.

Siobhan Maher's life had gone to hell after her husband was shot and killed. There was danger in being a cop's wife, always the threat of violence. "If it happens," she had thought, "I'll be ready for it. I'll be strong for the kids." And there were kids, six of them. Regan, the oldest girl, then Dylan, and Sean came soon after. She hoped they'd stop at three, but that wasn't what a good Irish Catholic family did. So, she had three more, the twins, Aoifa and Allison, and the baby, Liam. The Mahers struggled on a cop's salary, but one day as she was doing the check book, Siobhan found a thousand dollars she couldn't account for. She questioned Michael. All he would say is that God provides.

The month that Michael was murdered in his patrol car, the thousand from God stopped. It was just a policeman's pension and a one-time insurance payment in the savings now. Siobhan had done no more than raise the six kids; she had little time for anything else. Now she was faced with providing for them, none out of the house and working yet, all still in school. "God only gives us the burdens we can shoulder," she told herself, but her burden kept getting heavier. She got a job working as a receptionist at a dentist's office. After mass one day, Father Sweeney had cajoled Brian Mc Sorley to hire her as his dental receptionist. It was a dull lifeless job. The only thing that took the edge off her long days was the shot of Old Bushmills she drank at night when all the kids were asleep. Then she looked in the mirror. "Sagging breasts, baggy eyes, and spreading backside. Who"ll want me now? Am I done with it all? Live like a fuckin' nun from now on."

One shot became a juice glass full. Finally, the bottle came out during the day, hidden in various places, including the lower drawer of her office desk. "God woman! I'm a dentist. Here you are chewing gum from the minute you get in 'til you leave." Dr. Mc Sorley wasn't happy with Siobhan, but he felt it his Catholic and civic duty to help the widowed wife of a fallen policeman, particularly an Irish one.

Regan Maher was a looker, a redhead with twinkling blues and an hour glass figure. She was very popular with the boys from Brooklyn Prep. Recently, she'd started seeing a senior track athlete and part-time DJ named Robbie Gaeta-Jones. Siobhan didn't know about Robbie. Regan was a Saint Saviour's girl and Robbie was a Brooklyn Prep guy. It was natural enough for kids from the two Catholic single sex high schools to pair off. Regan met Robbie in a burger joint where she waited tables after school. She gave her mother her wages to help out with the family, but kept the tips for herself.

Robbie, on the other hand, didn't work. He drove a little sky blue Miata. He dressed in stylish clothes, no Gap for him. He was into Manhattan fashion. He had the body for it. He was six feet one and only one hundred and sixty pounds, and those pounds were all sinewy muscle, befitting a distance runner. Regan and Robbie were an item. Everybody knew that but Siobhan, who still thought her daughter chaste and uninterested in boys, more set on her career goal of becoming a lawyer.

Robbie was in love with Regan. Regan thought she was in love with Robbie, but she held back some of herself. She was indoctrinated well by her mother, so she always doubted the intentions of the boys who flocked to her. "They just want to get in your pants, daughter," her mother always told her when the subject of boys came up between them.

Robbie showered Regan with presents, some so expensive she was embarrassed to show them to her family, so she hid them in her dresser drawer: a Tiffany solitaire diamond pendant, a Cartier watch, a Fendi bag, a Hermes scarf. Robbie told her he would give her anything she wanted if she would just be his.

One day he asked her, "Rey, if you could have anything, anything at all, what would it be? I'd find it and get it for you."

"You really want to know?"

"Yeah, really."

"I'd like to know who murdered my father and made my mother age years before her time, made her a lush."

"Your dad was a cop, right?"

"I told you the story."

"Give me a couple of days. I'll find out."

"Sure, you'll find out what the cops couldn't. Do you know how hard they work to find out who killed one of their own? And you, a high school boy, think you can do better? Well, go for it, boyo, as my dad used to say."

The Gaeta in Robbie's hyphenated last name was his mother's maiden name. She was the only daughter of the Mafioso, Crazy Bobby Gaeta. Carol Gaeta prepped at the best schools in New York and married into a banking family. She'd cut off ties with her father when her mother died of a sudden stroke five years earlier. Robbie barely knew his grandfather, but he knew what he was. So, Robbie worked the channels back to his grandad, and found a very receptive man, who was more than happy to give Robbie the name of Jimmy Diamond or Jimmy Diaz as he was once known. Robbie gave that name to Regan.

They were sitting on a blanket, having a picnic lunch in East River Park on the Manhattan side of the Williamsburg Bridge. "Rey, Jimmy Diamond."

"Jimmy who?"

"The guy who killed your father."

"Seriously?"

"I wouldn't kid about something like this. I got it from a reliable source, my Mafia grandad."

"A guy named Jimmy Diamond killed my father, but why?"

"That I don't know, but I can tell you that he

was born Jimmy Diaz and he changed his name to
Diamond several years ago."

"Jimmy Diamond was Jimmy Diaz?"

"Yeah, so what are you gonna do?"

"Tell the police. There are still one or two who
stop over now and then to look in on the family. But
I won't tell my mother. She has enough on her plate
as it is."

"What do you want, Rey?"

"Justice for all of us. When our dad was
murdered, our family went to hell. We're still there. I
go months at a time without a smile from my
brothers and sisters."

CHAPTER EIGHTEEN:
Jailed

Regan Maher had been as good as her word. She spoke to Gerald McCann, who kept in touch with the Maher family. McCann spoke to Murphy and Casserly. The game was on again. They had enough to bring Jimmy Diamond aka Jimmy Diaz in for questioning.

Crazy Bobby Gaeta said he would testify if given immunity. It was a big if, but the cops really wanted Jimmy. Gaeta's story was that Jimmy Diaz was once on his payroll, but he let him go because he was freelancing outside the family. Bobby said the word was that Diaz had done a cop on his own, something about payback. Gaeta said he brought Diaz to question him face to face. Diaz admitted killing the cop. He said he shot him in his squad car, was nobody's loss because the cop was dirty, and besides he hated Puerto Ricans. Diaz said he needed the extra money because he had a family now, and life was more expensive for four than for one alone.

Jimmy was home alone raking fall leaves when the NYPD squad car pulled into the driveway. Murphy and Casserly got out of the back. Two armed officers exited the front and held automatic rifles at the ready. Behind the first squad car was a second and a third. Jimmy knew it was serious. "Maybe it's my time," he said to himself.

"Jimmy Diaz, you are wanted for questioning in the death of Sargent Michael Maher of the New York Police Department," Murphy intoned. "Please get in the second car. Extend your hands to me so that I can put the cuffs on you." Jimmy complied.

"Can I at least call my wife and kids?"

"No, we will inform your family when we reach

One Police Plaza." So began Jimmy's dance through the process of questioning him, charging him, bringing him to trial, and convicting him of first degree murder in the death of Sargent Michael Maher. At least, the judge let him tell his story on the stand.

"I grew up with no one to teach me right from wrong. I found out quickly that if I didn't take care of myself, no one would. When I was little, I was brought up by my auntie, who dropped dead a few years later from working two jobs and raising a family on her own. What I could see in front of me was a life of misery unless I acted. I had no education, no job, no prospects. I lived a life in the streets. I did the worst you can do. I robbed. I pimped. I took someone's life. But that person is not me. Through my wife's love and support, I am a changed man. I am not that rudderless criminal Jimmy Diaz. I am Jimmy Diamond, a man with a family who loves him and who he loves more than life itself. I know I must pay for my crime and I do it willingly. My heart is sad, but it is still full of my family's love, and that's what I will cherish when I am sent away. I can't bring back

Sargent Maher and I am sincerely sorry for what I did to him and to his family."

When Jimmy stepped down, more than a few eyes in the courtroom were full of tears. People could see that he had changed. His defense was that he was not Jimmy Diaz any longer, but Jimmy Diamond, a family man, a good father and a good citizen, and he had been so for many years now. He testified that the Gaetas had set him up as their hit man, but Crazy Bobby Gaeta's testimony against him seemed to carry greater weight with the judge and jury. He pleaded guilty to the murder of Sargent Maher, and threw himself on the mercy of the court, against the best advice of counsel. The story was kept out of the papers and handled as swiftly as any trial and conviction that the backlogged New York City judicial system could manage.

For the positive change he made in his life and for his honesty, the jury did not recommend a life without parole sentence, much to the chagrin of the blue uniforms in attendance at sentencing. The judge followed the jury's will and sentenced Jimmy to life in prison. His family was at the sentencing too. They would no longer have a father for Maisie and Davie nor a husband for Star. At the trial, one odd event occurred. Maisie let out a scream when she saw Crazy Bobby Gaeta on the stand, "That's him. That man is a criminal. He hurt my father." She stood up and pointed to Gaeta. Her speech after nearly a year of silence stunned Star, Davie and Jimmy. Maisie turned to Jimmy, "My dad was nearly killed by that man. There were two others with him. I saw it all." She kept screaming, "I saw you" at Gaeta. Bailiffs removed her from the courtroom. Star rushed out of the courtroom after her daughter. Davie remained in the courtroom. He could not move. He was stunned by his sister's voice.

Jimmy Diamond began serving his life sentence the winter of that year in the Five Points Correctional Facility in Romulus, New York. Its library held three thousand volumes, and the possibility of engrossing Jimmy enough to keep his mind alive. Jimmy spent time outdoors in the agriculture and horticulture program. This was his life now, celibate and contemplative. There were others like him full of regret and remorse for the deeds they had done, and there were those who'd do them again if they ever got out.

Jimmy was allowed occasional conjugal visits with Star. One day, after he'd been in for over four years, he had such a visit. They sat opposite each other, separated by bulletproof glass, not that it was at all necessary in Jimmy's case.

"Jimmy, you're going to be a father. I knew a month or so ago but I was waiting to tell you face to face. And Jimmy, your son, because it is a boy; I just know it's a boy. Your son will lead the life that you wanted to lead, a life of love and family. Jimmy, I only wish the world could see you for who you really are. I love you, Jimmy, and I always will. The children miss you desperately. I, I…" And then she broke down, tears running down her face onto the black telephone that enabled prisoner and guest to communicate. On the other side of the phone line, Jimmy caught his breath and murmured, "I love you forever. I am so sorry to leave you this way. I can never make it up to you." And he began to weep as well, for perhaps the first time in his adult life.

Jimmy watched his wife walk out of the prison. He realized that it would be so much easier to forget that he had a family, a wife and a son and a daughter who loved him, who grieved for him inside a prison cell, and wanted no more than to have him back. He realized it would be easiest to forget, to save himself emotionally, yet he resolved never to forget who he had become, and to let that pain stab him again and again in his heart of hearts. It made him more than a convict in a prison jump suit. It made him a man with a broken heart.

James Jr. was born in Kingston Hospital. He came into the world at ten pounds, with ruddy cheeks and jet black hair. Star said the first time he opened his eyes he smiled at her. Star brought him to see his father every two weeks.

CHAPTER NINETEEN: Two Paths Converge

Johnny became more and more dependent on his sister and her daily pep talks to lift his spirits. Isabella installed him in her condo guest room, brought him shopping for clothes and cooked for him. She did so much solely for Johnny that she neglected her business responsibilities. And the board of Rosso International was not happy with her. In particular, the Japanese board member, Malcolm Ozu, a youngish man who spoke fluent English, was very critical of Isabella in the best of times. He had a razor sharp mind and tongue. Malcolm wasn't his real name. In Japanese, he was Ozu Makoto, but in a multinational corporation where English was the lingua franca, non-Japanese, gaijin felt more comfortable with someone named Malcolm than Makoto.

Malcolm Ozu was allegedly the grandson of a prominent *yakuza* clan, equivalent to the Japanese mafia. There were rumors about tattoos and a surgically-repaired little finger. But no one knew for sure. What was clear was that Malcolm Ozu was not happy with Rosso International's management in Japan. Genaro Rosso, Isabella's brother, was supervising Rosso International from his San Francisco office, but not present in Japan often enough for Ozu's liking.

All of this was on Isabella's mind when she thought of the business, but Johnny's fragile self-image was taking most of her time. She had to come to some sort of resolution with Johnny so that she could do her own work.

"Johnny, do you know, and I know it's hard to say sometimes, do you know what you want? What would make you happy?"

"I thought it was my dojo and following my sensei's teachings, but now I'm not so sure. I'm in a dark place, Isabella, and I feel bad because I have taken my main student, Marvin Reichman, with me into this dark place."

"Why? Isn't he running the dojo in Southampton?"

"He is, but he senses something isn't right, and .he is starting to move away from the path."

"What do you mean?"

"I've heard rumors that he has been using his skills for his own profit, acting as a bodyguard for the rich while neglecting his role as a teacher of aikido."

"What's wrong with that? I'm a businesswoman and profit is what I am after."

"Yes, I know, but the path of the peaceful warrior, of aikido is different. It is selfless."

"Are you?"

"Am I selfless? Perhaps not, and perhaps that is part of my problem. Maybe my true self isn't altruistic despite my choices in life so far: social worker and aikido instructor."

"You know, Johnny, I think you are right. I think you should take that as a starting point and see where it leads you. Self-discovery is a powerful tool."

"And where should I go? What is my next step?"

"Close the dojo, but make sure Marvin is settled. Strike out on your own again, but with some sense of a safe harbor."

"And where would my safe harbor be?"

"Here with me."

"With you?"

"Yes, it has become uncomfortably clear that I need some sort of protection both to discourage those who wish to see me come to harm and to protect me in the event that harm comes my way. You can do this. You can be my bodyguard."

Johnny didn't know how to respond, so he remained silent.

"Johnny?"

"Give me a day to think about this."

"Okay. Let me know tomorrow. I'll make you dinner and we can talk."

Isabella needed an intimate, someone she could speak to openly and plainly, and Johnny was a good listener. Because he taught a spiritual martial art, he had experience in the art of giving counsel. And Isabella needed that. She also needed someone to watch her back, to give her a sense that she was physically safe. As she thought about what had just transpired, she wondered whether she and Johnny were fated to be together. After all, he had been her social worker, purely by chance. By blood, he was her cousin. By adoption, he was her brother. Johnny was her responsibility as head of the Rosso clan.

While Isabella tried to solve her Johnny problem, Malcolm Ozu was creating another problem for her with the board. She learned of it when he called.

"Miss Rosso, may I ask when you are going to visit Japan? We, your Japanese partners, feel that we miss your presence. Genaro visits once a month, but we think this is not enough. Sales in Japan are not progressing.

We are losing markets for air cargo, for fine Italian wines and clothing. We need to rethink our presence in my country. We need a new direction. Rosso International must become more Japanese if it wishes to make a profit in Japan. If you do not take a greater interest, I am afraid I am going to ask the board to review your tenure as chairperson."

"I appreciate your frankness, Mr.Ozu. I do plan to visit Japan in the near future. You have my word. And I will do my best to secure Rosso International's interests there. You have every right to expect excellence of me as your chairperson. I hope to show you that excellence when I travel to Tokyo."

A general disquiet among board members occurred. No one had anticipated that Isabella would take things so directly into her own hands.

She had always relied upon the management of Rosso International, which included her brothers Gennaro and Gildo, to explore markets and look for ways to achieve new profit which fit into the context of the culture and country in which the company was active. Her hope was that the Rosso brain-trust in Japan, both foreign and Japanese, would begin a strong push into China. That effort seemed to have stalled. Perhaps she was not as up on things as she should be, and she blamed herself for it. She knew she had to make the trip to Japan a success. Malcolm Ozu was either looking to oust her and take her place or find someone he could control to do so. The corporation must remain under Rosso control.

CHAPTER TWENTY:
Confrontation

Johnny was anxious during the whole flight from JFK to Narita. He was in a new job, head of security for Rosso International and bodyguard to Isabella. He had installed Marvin as the new instructor at the Southampton dojo. Could he follow the path? He hadn't heard a word from Kobayashi Sen-Sei. Perhaps it was to be expected as the venerable aikido master spoke little English, and did not write it; he hardly spoke at all, even in Japanese. That was what Johnny remembered. He wondered if his sen-sei was still alive. In any case, he'd had to travel to Nara to pay his respects.

Isabella was not exactly anxious. She was rather anticipating her work in Japan, and aware that with all its modernization, Japan was still a male-dominated society when it came to business and power. She had also done her homework on Malcolm Ozu, and discovered that he was related to an old yakuza family, on his father's side. It was a family that had lost much of its power in Tokyo with the rise of the postwar generation. The old *oyabun*, the clan leader Ozu Masahiro, had a daughter, Sumi, who married a GI from the Bronx during the military occupation of the archipelago. Sumi kept the family name, gave birth to a son, her only child, named Osamu. He, in turn, married into a leading business family, one of the *zaibatsu*. When the conglomerate went belly up, Ozu Osamu placed his son and two daughters under the protection of a friend, a *wakagashira*, or lieutenant, in a yakuza clan, which had carved out a small niche in the Japanese entertainment industry. The three children were sent off to an international school in Switzerland. The understanding between the two families was that each child would serve the yakuza in some future way to repay the debt incurred by taking the children in and giving them an international education.

Ozu Makoto learned English, studied international law at the London School of Economics and had an internship with Citibank in Tokyo. He was, in this way, like many of the newly-educated yakuza young people, with a foot in two worlds, East and West. He was at once Malcolm Ozu and Ozu Makoto, a single body but two minds, one at home in the Rosso International boardroom and one within the structure of the yakuza clan.

Malcolm Ozu was a hard-working lawyer, international in outlook, interested in the latest designer fashion and luxury cars, but not focused only on material success. He was also fluent in the language of literature, cinema, technology and world politics. Ozu was part of the new world elite, who moved easily from country to country and culture to culture. To his knowledge of English, he added conversational French and Spanish, a reading knowledge of German, and he was working on Italian. Ozu was no inward-looking Japanese.

Ozu Makoto was thoroughly Japanese, aware of the debt he owed to the yakuza family that fostered him, focused on duty, focused on hierarchy, and convinced of the idea that Japan, a superior nation, had for too long suffered at the heavy, meaty hand of the West. His home was luxurious, ten thousand square feet in Tokyo, a size to startle the average Japanese.

Yet Ozu lived a traditional Japanese home life. His wife was devoted to the education of his son and daughter. Not a word of English passed between the couple although both were fluent speakers. His family dressed in traditional Japanese clothing and celebrated all the traditional Japanese holidays, but especially *tenno no tanjobi*, the emperor's birthday.

Malcom Ozu. Ozu Makoto. He was of two minds, two names, two cultures, in opposition to each other in their values, ethics, and mores.

He was an ideal addition to the board of Rosso International. Indeed, Isabella Rosso, the current chairwoman's adoptive mother, knew Ozu's family from post-war business dealings that the Rosso family had with yakuza families in Tokyo.

She knew of the three Ozu children, and before she died, she recommended to her daughter that she recruit Malcolm Ozu to the board of Rosso International. Ozu, then only twenty-nine years old, had already been made CFO of the Ae Corporation in Tokyo, a new firm that had achieved rapid success in real estate investment in Japan, Korea and the United States. When Isabella took over the chair from her mother, one of her first moves was to recruit Malcolm Ozu to the board of Rosso International. Now, however, Ozu opposed Isabella and was building a coalition to back his move for the chair of the multinational.

Malcolm Ozu was a new type of gangster, *keizai yakuza*, expert in white collar crime. Ozu dressed in double breasted Italian suits, wore designer sun glasses, and carried the latest I-Phone and Macbook in his Gucci leather briefcase. He was tanned, tall and good-looking. He had no tattoos and, despite rumors to the contrary, still had all five fingers on both hands.

His exquisite business cards in a gold case identified him as Chief Financial Officer of Ae Industries and a board member of Rosso International. Ozu read The Wall Street Journal, The Economist, The Financial Times, and monitored CNBC every day.

While Rosso International was a working multinational corporation, Ae Industries was nothing of the sort. There was no steel and glass building. The Ae Corporation existed only on paper. The corporation was a yakuza invention that laundered money, extracted loans they would never repay, and invested in inflated real estate. The extent of criminal involvement in the Japanese economy was such that when the economy tanked in the latter part of the twentieth century, people started referring to the yakuza recession.

In post-war Japan, politics, business and crime have had a long and close relationship. Despite maintaining the veneer of a modern businessman, Ozu was yakuza. That was his power base and the reason that he was able to succeed as he had. When layer upon layer was peeled away, what remained was criminal activity. Ozu's support team of yakuza at the Ae Corporation was expert in the art of '*jiage*', persuading recalcitrant property owners to sell their property. This they did by using terror – late night visits from yakuza, dead cats on doorsteps, threatening phone calls. Personally, Ozu worked another scam. Japan had a tangled web of regulations and laws pertaining to business transactions, and nearly every company broke the law in some way. Ozu sought out companies that he could extort. His payoff was in stock, and therefore he gained influence. He was thus able to control such companies by being 'appointed' to their boards. This is what he had in mind when he was asked to join the board of Rosso International. It was a gift that fell into his lap. Almost too good to be true. And with a woman as board chair!

Ozu's first move was to summon Gennaro Rosso to a meeting while his sister, the corporation chairperson, cooled her heels in her hotel room. Isabella, Johnny and Gennaro were staying at the Mandarin Oriental in Nihonbashi, the Tokyo business district. Ozu proposed that Gennaro and he get massages in the hotel spa. "A good way to begin a corporate visit," he told Gennaro over the phone. On their way out of the spa, Ozu asked Gennaro to wait for him outside. He then quickly phoned Isabella and asked her to meet him at the spa. Isabella thought it strange to meet there, but she agreed. A few minutes later, as she was exiting the elevator, she saw Gennaro and Ozu, hair still damp and bodies glowing a bit from massage.

"Malcolm. It's been a while. I didn't know that you and Gennaro were having massages," she said, extending her hand to Ozu. She tried to smile, but inside she was boiling at this slight, unintended or not. Ozu's first call should have been to her. They both knew that.

Ozu did not take her hand, but bowed instead. "I thought it a good idea to start off our business meetings with some relaxation, so I asked Gennaro to join me in getting a massage. Naturally, I couldn't ask you to do the same." And he smiled at her.

"Naturally," Isabella replied.

The first meeting was over dinner. Ozu and the Rossos had agreed to set out an agenda for the next few days in a convivial atmosphere. They had a table for four at Sense, the French cuisine restaurant in the hotel. The view of Tokyo was exquisite as was the food and wine. Ozu was charming. Johnny said little. Gennaro was painting a rosy picture of Rosso successes in Japan. Isabella tried to read Ozu, tried to read the message he was sending.

"Isabella, I hope you are finding your suite up to your high standards. I know everything that you do is first class, perfect, nearly. Is it not?"

"I would just say, Malcolm, that I enjoy everything in life that is done well, don't you?"

"But of course. And that makes me wonder just a bit."

"About what?"

"Our business venture here in Tokyo, and in Seoul, and in Beijing. The truth is that those three cities are more and more at the center of world business and trade, don't you think? And while Tokyo has been less than ideal for business these days, the other two markets are expanding. And so, I believe we should too."

"We have Gennaro and we have you. Do we need more? More of a presence in Korea and China?"

"Undoubtedly, we need a staff and a larger presence in both countries.

We also need someone with a visceral understanding of Eastern culture and language to oversee these operations. I believe we need to add two board members, one from each country. Our future success lies in East Asia."

"This wasn't part of the memo I got when I told you I was coming."

"Ah, yes. Well, it is something better broached in person, I believe."

And he smiled at each of them as if to establish that they all agreed on this.

Isabella was taken by surprise. "Surely, this is something for the board meeting, which is not until Monday."

"I believe we can act and then get the rest of the board to agree to what already has taken place."

"You mean make a move without board approval and then expect it afterwards?"

"Precisely."

"I'm afraid I can't agree. And anyway, who would this one person be who really understands East Asia? No one, but you, I would assume. And who would choose the board members from Korea and China? Again, you. Am I correct?"

"Yes, Isabella, you are quite correct indeed." Once more, Ozu smiled at everyone.

"This cannot happen," Isabella spoke slowly, but with emphasis on each word. She would not allow Ozu to rattle her. "Please excuse me, gentlemen. I need to make a phone call. Dinner was excellent. Why don't you three have a brandy in the bar? I'll catch up later."

At the bar, Ozu ordered a Hennessey for himself. "What will you have gentlemen?" he asked Gennaro and Johnny.

"Chivaz on the rocks," replied Gennaro.

"Just a Perrier or Pellegrino," answered Johnny.

"You don't drink, Johnny?"

"Not much."

"Is that because you are an aikido sen-sei? You want to set a good example? Clean living?"

"Not really. It's just me. I was never a drinker."

"I'd like you two to come to my home this evening. We'll leave Isabella to her own devices. It sounds like she wanted some alone time, no?"

Johnny was surprised by the invitation. He wasn't used to a Japanese inviting him home at first meeting. "It's getting late, Mr. Ozu."

"Malcom, please."

"Malcolm, perhaps tomorrow or after the board meeting?"

"Don't you say, 'Strike while the iron is hot'? What's wrong with a few hours of simple diversion. You and I can work out a little. I am sure, Johnny, that you miss the contact of aikido. Gennaro can be our referee, so to speak."

"Sure," Gennaro agreed. "I'd like to see your home. I've heard that you have a collection of samurai armor."

"Word does get around. You are more than welcome to see it, Gennaro."

"Well, okay," Johnny gave in to Ozu. Japanese hospitality once offered was not to be declined. That he knew. Besides, he thought it might help his sister in her dealings with Ozu.

The three men arrived in a chauffeured Bentley to the Ozu home. It was a walled property with several small Japanese gardens between the entrance gate and the main house. The last of these was a gravel and stone Zen garden, recently swept and geometrically pleasing to the eye. Johnny admired it whereas it puzzled Gennaro, who had never developed an understanding of the *wa* of such a landscape.

Inside the mansion, Ozu played host, escorting the two men to a large tatamied room that served as a personal dojo for Ozu. There were samurai suits of armor draped on mannequins spaced around the room. On the walls hung martial arts weapons: short bows, throwing blades, chains, and three types of Japanese swords: *katana, wakizashi,* and *tanto.* There were also *bokken* of different sizes for practicing the martial art of kendo.

Ozu and Johnny had changed into *kendo-gi,* black jackets and black wide legged trousers. Each wore a mask to protect the face. Each had a wooden practice sword, a bokken, in hand. They began to spar. Johnny easily parried Ozu's assaults, but this only made Ozu try harder with greater frequency.

"You are quite good, Johnny, a credit to your

sen-sei. But, let's have a practice match, the first one to two valid body strikes wins."

"I am sorry, Ozu-san, but I think it is time for Gennnaro and me to leave."

"This cannot be. I have invited you here, and now you refuse my request. Gennaro, will you take Johnny's place? I can teach you how to do kendo."

Gennaro Rosso was built squat and strong, and he was a dedicated body builder. He wasn't a martial arts practitioner, but he couldn't say no when he thought his masculinity was being called into question. "Sure. Why not?" he replied as he changed into the *keikogi* and *hakama*.

For the next fifteen minutes, Ozu slowly humiliated Gennaro Rosso by teaching him a strike move, then parrying Gennaro's attempt to use it. Instead Ozu struck back, inflicting pain. Johnny knew what was happening. Ozu was using Gennaro to provoke him into a match. Finally, he could take no more.

"Ozu-san, perhaps it would be better for me to continue. Let's give Gennaro a rest."

Gennaro was sweating and as he took off his jacket, one could see red welts all over his shoulders, arms, and torso. He was also steaming mad, ready to fight Ozu hand to hand. Johnny took up the bokken.

Ozu quickly scored a point as Johnny was calculating how to end the match without both of them losing face. He was thus not focused on the opponent in front of him. The match continued. Johnny quickly scored a point on Ozu. "Shall we stop here, Ozu-san?" Johnny asked hoping to save face for them both.

"No, let us see who the better man is," he answered.

Johnny reluctantly continued. He then dispatched Ozu. His second point won the match. Ozu threw down the bokken. He left the dojo without a word to either Johnny or Gennaro. The two men quietly exited the room as if in a haze of unreality occasioned by Ozu's abrupt departure. They were met by Ozu's chauffeur, who drove them back to the hotel. There was no bidding of good night. They would not see their host until the board meeting that Monday.

Malcolm Ozu made his pitch to the board at the Monday meeting. He was dressed in a navy blue worsted tropical suit, with red tie and white shirt. His outfit signaled his desire for power.

"My blood is that of a Japanese. I know my country. I know its people. I know its markets. I acknowledge a special bond with the people of Korea, the people of China, and the people of Vietnam. We were at one time all Confucian societies under the umbrella of imperial China. First, we Japanese diverged. Then the Vietnamese, and finally the Koreans. Yes, we have fought each other over the course of our histories, but it has been the fight of a family. We share certain things that the West does not. We revere age. We honor the scholar and the teacher. We see honor and loyalty as the hallmarks of a great society. We value family. We place the group above the individual. We value consistency. We value the ancients. We look to them for guidance.

You may say, 'But wait, modern Japan is nothing like that. Japanese are materialistic. They want the latest technology. They even throw out last year's television because it is out of date. Japanese imitate the West and seek the material goods and cultural capital that the West possesses.'

And to this I say, time. Time will tell. We have been in a Western dominated epoch since the Meiji Restoration, since Perry's ship forced Japan to "open" to the West, which really meant allowing Japan to be exploited by the West. Japan is much older than her contact with the West. The bonds she shares with other Asian countries are much older than any bonds she might have with the West. We need these new board members.

But my message is not meant to drive a wedge between West and East on the board of Rosso International. Instead it is to proclaim that the future of world markets is here in the East and that it will take an Asian to properly interact with those markets.

Therefore, my first point is that this corporation needs to expand its membership to include one representative from Korea and a second from China. Next, I humbly submit myself as the person, given the guidance and advice of the members of this board, to lead this company into the future as its chair."

And with that, Malcolm Ozu ended his argument in favor of his replacing Isabella Rosso as chair of the board of Rosso International. The board had already decided that Asian markets needed more attention and analysis than Gennaro's twice monthly trips and Ozu's other responsibilities had been able to give them. What they did not anticipate was that Ozu would make a bid to take the chair away from Isabella Rosso. What they did not know was that Ozu's yakuza family had purchased a majority share of stock in three companies under the Rosso International umbrella: Rosso Wines, Rosso Foods, and Rosso Transportation.

It was Isabella's turn.

"I thank Mr. Ozu for his directness and sincerity. I agree that we need to pay more attention to our markets in East Asia. We have made a start in this direction over the past few years, and I anticipate that we will increase our presence one hundred percent within the next five years. I also think it would be a good idea to expand the board to nine members from its current seven, searching for a suitable match in Korea and China. Where I must disagree with Mr. Ozu is on the question of the chair's leadership and personal qualities. Rosso International is just that, international. Because it does business all over the world, it cannot have as chair, a person so focused on only one part of that world, albeit an expanding one as far as markets are concerned. I believe my tenure as chair has brought prosperity to all the businesses under our corporate umbrella. The facts and figures speak to that. I feel that I have acquitted your faith in me as board chairperson, and I intend to continue in that role. I ask the board for a vote of confidence to come at the end of our proceedings this week. Thank you."

And with that, Isabella took her seat. Ozu did not look at her, but seemed a little less assured as he sat there and tried to gauge the effect of Isabella's presentation on the board members. The board would not meet again until Thursday. This was to allow board members a little time to enjoy Japan before serious decisions were made.

Tuesday morning was a bright autumn day with a tall blue sky. Isabella proposed to her brothers to travel by bullet train to Kobe and Nara. She wanted Johnny to know that she valued his time in Japan and his intimate knowledge of Japanese culture. The trip included touring the famous temples of Kyoto and the deer park of Nara. They would sleep in Japanese inns, eat Japanese style, and generally make themselves open to the people and culture. Johnny wanted to contact his sen-sei in Nara, and that was another reason for the trip south.

Johnny took a train to Nara ahead of Isabella and Gennaro, who were staying in Kyoto for the night. He went directly to Kobashi Sen-Sei's dojo in the foothills of Wakakusayama, where he learrned that

235

the old master had died the year before. None of the present residents of the dojo knew Johnny. He wandered around and watched the aikido training. He smiled to himself to think of the difficult time he had when he first came to the master's dojo. And he thought of how wonderful it became for him, how it had given his life meaning. He also regretted not trying harder to maintain contact with Kobayashi. Now he couldn't. Johnny was about to leave when he ran into a young man who was once a sort of secretary to the master. He looked at Johnny.

"Anata wa Jah nee sen-sei desuka?" (Are you Johnny Sen-Sei?)

"Hai, so, desu." (Yes, I am)

And with that he was given an envelope sealed with the master's seal. In it he read, "Johnny, I have given you everything I could give. Even though you were a foreigner, you became a son to me. I deeply wish that you take over the dojo here in Nara. I had this letter translated for you because I want you to understand clearly.

Signed,

Kobayasi Isamu"

Johnny folded the letter and put it in his coat pocket. He thanked the young man who had given him Kobayashi's letter.

"Sayonara," he said as he turned to leave. Inside, he felt confusion grow. "Am I to be here to follow my master or am I to be with Isabella?"

Later he found himself wandering through the deer park, feeding the once-sacred deer. He had no idea how he had gotten there. It was dark when he bought a ticket on the Kintetsu line for Kyoto.

Isabella had taken to the routine of a traditional Japanese *ryokan*.

She bathed and went directly to her room to sleep. She was comfortable under the quilt. As she lay down on the hard pillow, her neck fitting its contour snugly, she looked at the moonlight which played upon the *shoji* sliding doors to her room. She drifted off to sleep. Around midnight, a figure all in black silently slid the shoji doors apart, then closed them.

The figure approached Isabella, and quickly put a chloroform-laden cloth over her nose and mouth until she lost consciousness. Then he partially disrobed, unbuttoned Isabella's pajama top and pulled down her pajama bottoms. He thrust hard enough to draw some drops of blood. He finished, clothed himself and was gone.

In the morning, Isabella at first had no idea of what had transpired the night before. It was only when she felt between her legs and touched her sore vagina that she began to panic. She looked down to see crusted white stains on her quilt. She touched them. "It couldn't be," she thought. "I was alone all night. I slept through. What happened?" She later discovered some blood stains on her pajama bottoms. A sense of panic claimed her mind.

She felt a strong need to bathe again. So she did. Still the feeling that something was very wrong would not pass. Johnny, Gennaro and she toured Nara that morning, but she could not take interest in anything she saw. Johnny noticed this and asked if something was wrong. She told him that she didn't know. The brothers and sister took a bullet train back to Tokyo that evening. At the Mandarin Oriental, Gennaro and Johnny went to their rooms and Ella to hers. At one o'clock in the morning, Isabella called Johnny.

"Johnny, I've been raped," she cried.

CHAPTER TWENTY-ONE:
Machinations

It was too late to ascertain by the normal forensic parameters whether Isabella had been raped, but a new French test, valid up to two days after the rape, could detect Y chromosome cells even in the absence of sperm. This test was made available to Isabella in confidence. It indicated the presence of male cells. Isabella had been raped.

The next question was who did it and why. It didn't take long for Isabella and Johnny to suspect Ozu. "It was either him or some goon he hired," Johnny said. "Just another way to try to humiliate us."

Johnny kept his next thought to himself. What better way for Ozu to indicate his superiority over a woman than to take her by force? Of course, he would deny having anything to do with it.

"We've got to get him to admit that he or one of his men did it."

Thursday afternoon at two o'clock the board was scheduled to meet at a conference room in the Mandarin Oriental. The original board had been put together by the late Isabella Rosso. She selected her son Gennaro. Then she asked Abraham Aiello to serve. She enlisted the family lawyer, Gerry Lucas. She needed three more members, so she looked to France, where Gildo had begun to manage the family interests. Rather than choosing another son, she asked Gildo to choose the Frenchman he trusted most in his dealings. Thus came Guy De Longue, a Sorbonne-educated scholar and a leading globalist in France. De Longue was all for eliminating impediments to trade and for the free movement of people across national borders. He was also an astute businessman who grew Rosso interests in France and northern Europe. The sixth board member was Malcolm Ozu, and the seventh was Allen Dale, a British investment banker, who was level headed and thoughtful, and whom the older Isabella often leaned on for advice. The only changes made were the younger Isabella taking her mother's place, and Lucas stepping down in favor of Chi Kai Won, a Chinese merchant from Shanghai, who was vital to Rosso International's success in China. If Ozu had his way, there would be two more members, one Chinese and one Korean, and Ozu would be voted chair with Isabella losing her seat on the board. This would upset the balance.

Isabella could always depend on Aiello, Gennaro, and De Longue to support her while Dale often did, and Chi and Ozu often did not. Adding another Chinese and a Korean, both presumably under Ozu's control, would not immediately change the balance of power, but would likely do so in the future. Both Aiello and Dale had indicated they would retire within the next year. If Ozu became chair, he could stack the deck in his favor, gaining two seats and thus a potential majority of six. Ozu's major holdings in Rosso companies would enable him to manipulate shareholder meetings. With Isabella out, Gennaro would be the only authentic Rosso voice on the board.

The board voted unanimously, seven to zero, to add two new members, one from Seoul and one from Beijing, making two members from that country, befitting its size and importance on the world scene. The board also voted to have Malcolm Ozu recruit the candidate from Korea while Isabella was responsible for finding a candidate from China. Then the vote was called on Ozu's proposal to replace Isabella. Gennaro, Aiello and Isabella voted against the proposal. Chi, De Longue and Ozu voted for it. De Longue's vote surprised the Rossos. He had almost always been on their side of an issue. Dale was the deciding vote. He submitted his resignation rather than vote either way.

The board now had only six members, and was at a stalemate.

As chair, it was up to Isabella to find a way out of the impasse. She made a motion to table the question of who would be chair until three new board members could be added. She further proposed that a subcommittee of De Longue, Aiello and Chi find a replacement member for Allen Dale while she recruited a second Chinese board member and Ozu a Korean board member. This motion passed four to two, Ozu and Chi in opposition. The new board members would be identified by the close of the meeting a week from that Thursday. The meeting ended in anticipation of what would come. Johnny, Gennaro and Isabella left together.

Two men Johnny didn't know walked directly into his path, separating him from Gennaro and Isabella. At the same time, Ozu brushed past Isabella, He turned to her and said, "Isabella, how did you find the ryokan in Kyoto? I trust you slept well."

Gennaro heard what Ozu said. Anger surged through his body. He grabbed Ozu around the chest and squeezed as if to empty him of life. Ozu was unable to escape the iron hold of Gennaro, but after a few seconds, Gennaro quickly let go, sliding down to the floor, the wound from a small sword gushing blood from his back. Ozu's crew had rescued him. Five yakuza made a protective circle around Ozu as he sprinted for his Bentley. Meanwhile, Johnny ran to Gennaro's side, covering the wound with his jacket, pressing down hard to slow the blood loss.

"Isabella! Come quickly!" he screamed to his sister, "Gennaro's been stabbed." Ella came running, while Johnny dialed his cell phone for an ambulance.

"What happened? How did this happen to Gennaro?"

"I think it was one of Ozu's crew," replied Johnny, "and I expect to find out."

CHAPTER TWENTY-TWO:
Decisions

Johnny hadn't dreamed of the redhead in years, he thought. But that night, as Gennaro lay in a hospital bed with Johnny sleeping at his side, the redhead appeared again. This time Johnny dreamed of a tropical isle with a lone figure looking out to sea, her back turned away from Johnny. He slowly approached her. *"What's wrong?"* *he asked.*

"Oh it's you again." *the redhead replied over her shoulder.* *"You've never gotten the job done, have you?"* *And with those words, she began to sob, her back shaking violently as she did so. "Will I always be a prisoner here? Can't you do something?"*

Johnny put a hand on her shoulder and gently turned her

around to face him. "This time I promise I will..." But before he could finish, the redhead's face became Isabella's face. Johnny was speechless.

Then he awoke.

Gennaro's wound was serious, but not critical. He would need to stay in the hospital for a week minimum. This meant it was not clear whether he could attend the board meeting scheduled for a week ahead. Isabella Rosso had inherited her place as board chair, but she was a natural leader. She conducted affairs in a direct, straightforward manner. For a motion to pass, four of the seven board members needed to be present and to vote in favor of it. Initially, the late Isabella Rosso had no trouble getting her way because she appointed all the members for the board at the time it formed. However, now the corporation had gone public. Shares were available. Shareholders voted in board members. This was largely a pro forma exercise as there were no candidates in opposition.

Ozu's numerous shares in three Rosso businesses

meant that he could sway voting for board members.
He would control the new board member from
Korea. He assumed the Rossos would do the same
for the new Chinese board member. What wasn't
clear is what the committee charged with finding
Allen Dale's replacement would do.

The night before the meeting, Isabella received a
phone call from Allen Dale.

"Isabella, I need to explain myself. I resigned
because I simply do not have enough energy for the
fight ahead. I fear the board of the corporation is
becoming overly politicized to the detriment of its
primary goal of doing business and making money.
You and Ozu will inevitably lock horns, and I fear it
will be a fight to the death. One of you will ultimately
go. I didn't want to be there for that to happen. I
wish you the best. You've been a worthy successor to
your mother, and the model of an ethical
businesswoman. Goodbye."

And with that, he hung up. Isabella had done
nothing but listen. Her thoughts turned to the

committee of three. They were to identify a replacement for Dale by the day of the meeting. Who would it be? That night Isabella dreamed that her mother had returned to take Dale's position. She woke up sure that her dream had meaning for the day. It gave her hope.

Gennaro was not released from the hospital. Thus, there were only five board members on that Thursday. Still four would need to vote yes for a motion to pass. Ozu introduced a former member of the KCIA and present CEO of Korean International, a trading company. His name was Kim Young Chul. Ozu extoled the virtues of Mr. Kim as a forward-looking businessman who was interested in pan-Asian trade. "Ideal for Rosso International," vouched Ozu. Next, Isabella introduced Chou Hua whom Gildo had scouted on Isabella's behalf and recommended to her as an innovative businesswoman from Shanghai who was attempting to blend the Chinese 'we' with the Western 'I' into a new organizational model acceptable to East and West, a model which stressed the inclusion of women at all levels of the corporate structure. The vote was three to two in favor of Chou Hua. Isabella, Aiello, and De Longue voted yes. Ozu and Chi voted no. The vote for Kim was two to two, with Isabella and Aiello voting against the Korean. De Longue abstained from voting on the candidate. Thus, the meeting was at a stalemate. Each candidate needed four votes.

Then Isabella introduced Allen Dale's replacement. Her name was Anna Park. She was a second-generation Australian of Korean origin. She was a hi tech entrepreneur who had created four successful social media sites in Australia, with one of them, *My Story*, going global. She would act as a replacement until her candidacy was voted on by shareholders. As a replacement, she was entitled to vote at that meeting. She had been brought up to speed and knew the candidates and their supporters. The result was a revote in which both Kim and Chou were approved by four to two.

Ozu's bid for the chairmanship was tabled until the next meeting in New York City in three months. Isabella had some breathing room. Shareholders approved Park, Kim and Chou. The board had seven members again. Gennaro was released from the hospital ten days after he was admitted. He had pain in his back and side. He was short of breath, but he was alive with one thought in his head, revenge against Ozu.

Johnny was thinking about what Ozu had done to Isabella and Gennaro, what he had tried to do to Johnny: insults, physical assault, overt antipathy, mocking compliments. Johnny was the only one who had gotten the upper hand against Ozu. He found a weakness in Ozu's pride. In defeat, Ozu would not acknowledge Johnny's superior skill at kendo. Johnny thought he might use this in some way. But he was cautious. He remembered an old saying he had heard his mother use. "Revenge is a dish best served cold." Both Isabella and Gennaro were burning up inside over Ozu. Johnny could put a little distance between himself and their foe. He thought that he was in the best position to call Ozu to account for what he had done to them. He believed that his dream had called him to action. What would he do?

CHAPTER TWENTY-THREE:
Plotting Payback

Everyone, even yakuza, has enemies. This was the principle by which Johnny would get revenge for his family. He stayed in Tokyo another two weeks after Isabella had gone back to New York and Gennaro to San Francisco. His Japanese was good enough to read the newspaper and handle most conversations. So he read the newspaper for any information about Ozu, the yakuza family that supported him, and Ae Corporation. He contacted associates in the aikido community to see what he could find about Ozu, whether they knew Ozu and whether they knew his enemies. Johnny assumed that

253

Ozu had some training in aikido from the evening of the kendo match at his house.

Eventually, Johnny found out a few things he thought he could use. First, Ozu had an unnatural fear of water. He would not go near a boat or even to the seashore. Second, Ozu was in debt to a *wakagashira* in the Sumiyoshi-kai of Tokyo. It was the yakuza lieutenant who raised him and his sisters and paid for their education, and now wanted payback for his years of support. Ozu's sisters were both graduate students in the States and didn't have much money. Ozu supported them. He also paid a monthly sum to his yakuza 'uncle', but had a much larger debt hanging over him. It was a debt that the uncle, who had set up Ozu in a yakuza-owned business, wanted paid by the end of the year. The third piece of information that Johnny learned was that Ozu had a mistress that his wife didn't know about.

Johnny hired a bar hostess to call the wife. He posed as a wealthy American businessman and went to a bar in the Ginza where he knew *gaijin* were welcome and the girls were English-speaking. His hostess, a girl from Hokkaido, 'Missu Yamaguchi', thought Johnny was a great kidder. He made her laugh by imitating clueless gaijin who wanted to meet Japanese women. He told her jokes in Japanese and English. Then after a few rounds of champagne for Missu Yamaguchi and Perrier for himself, he proposed that they play a joke on his good Japanese friend. He got Missu Yamaguchi to call Ozu's wife and pretend that she was waiting for him at the Bar Musashi and expecting him to bring the present he had promised her. Then she hung up. Aiko, Ozu's wife, immediately called her husband, and accused him of lying to her. She wanted to know who his mistress was. Aiko was not an average Japanese housewife and mother. She was the daughter of a Sumiyoshi-kai *kyo-dai*, an elder brother. To anger Aiko was to bring the wrath of a yakuza senior to Ozu. Ozu had not yet been inducted into the gang. He had yet to drink sake with the *oyabun*, the leader. He risked everything if he upset Aiko and her father.

Johnny's second act of revenge was not easy to pull off. He had to find a way to discover Ozu's worth. He knew an American reporter for a Japanese newspaper, a reporter who covered the Tokyo crime beat. He had run into the man, a Texan named James Sherman, at aikido meets over the years. Sherman was an amateur practitioner of aikido and he admired Johnny for his character and his ability as a disciple of Kobayashi Sen-Sei. Johnny and Sherman were sitting at a coffee shop in Shinjuku.

"James, how do you get your inside information on yakuza bank accounts?"

"Why the interest?"

"Can I just say that I have a very good reason for wanting to know one man's finances? He is someone who has wronged my family, bringing harm to my sister and brother."

"Hmmm. Whom did you have in mind?"

"Ozu Makoto, known to Westerners as Malcolm Ozu."

"I know him well. I've shared more than one beer with him. He is about the most polished of the

Sumiyoshi-kai, almost like a mouthpiece for that gang. If you give me a day or two, maybe I can find out what he's worth and where he's hiding it. But then you'll owe me big time. How about a free lesson?"

"Deal," answered Johnny.

In two days, they met again. Sherman handed Johnny a flash drive. "It'll make interesting reading," he said as he handed it over.

Johnny took it to his hotel room, opened his lap top, inserted the flash drive, and read the contents. He made a copy to his lap top and then sent one each to Isabella and Gennaro with a note that it should be kept quiet for now.

The note read, "Ozu Makoto supposedly owns a beach front property in Hawaii, an apartment house just outside of Tokyo, fifty million yen in stock in Rosso Wines, Rosso Foods, and Rosso Air. He has about one million dollars' worth of stock in other U.S. and Japanese companies. He has nearly that much in the bank in checking and savings. However, the kicker is that the Sumiyoshi-kai controls Ozu and can call in the whole lot as debt repayment if they want to. Ozu has to be very careful to play the game by Sumiyoshi rules. If not, not only his fortune, but his life might end."

Johnny would hold this information until the right time came to exploit it. Most interesting was Ozu's fear of water. Apparently, he had nearly drowned in the ocean when he was a toddler, and from that time on had never so much as stuck a toe in the surf. "This information might give me the context for our final revenge," Johnny thought. "Everything is in the timing."

CHAPTER TWENTY-FOUR:
Things Begin to Turn

It was mid-March. The cherry blossoms were in bloom. Johnny knew that to a Japanese sensibility, there is no more beautiful expression of the natural world than the blossoms on a cherry tree and their subsequent fall to the ground. They represent the fleetingness of beauty and of life, and since they are a natural phenomenon, the acceptance of destiny. It is the blossom's destiny to fall and die, just as it is man's destiny to enter life and pass away. For the Japanese, there is no greater pleasure than picnicking under a cherry tree in full blossom. This custom of *hanami* is part of Japanese culture and history, dating from the eighth century Nara period and continuing today. During the Second World War, kamikaze pilots and dead warrior souls became closely linked to the cherry blossom.

Johnny took Isabella and Gennaro on a hanami. Their lunch was cold chicken, potato salad and a good prosecco that Johnny had found in a small Italian shop in Shibuya. Johnny had prepared the lunch, guided the viewing of the cherry blossoms, and now it was time for him to lay out the plan for the family's revenge against Ozu.

"Isabella. Gennaro. It is nearly time for our revenge against Ozu.

My first question to you is, "Do you really want revenge and do you believe it is worth the trouble it will cause?" My second question is, "What is our goal at the upcoming board meeting if not to regain control and order?" My third question to you is, "Given the first two concerns, revenge and restoring order, do we believe them to be of equal importance?"

Gennaro spoke first. "I want blood. Blood for blood. For what he did to me and to Isabella."

"Thus, revenge, Gennaro. And you, Isabella?"

"I'm not sure that revenge is our priority. Believe me I hate Ozu and what he did to me, but I think maybe our best revenge is regaining control of the corporation our mother began and then getting rid of Ozu as a board member."

"So we are not of one mind," Johnny replied. "Then we need to think a little more until we find a consensus."

The discussion eventually centered on wresting control of Rosso International from Ozu despite Gennaro's desire for blood.

"I think we have an understanding now," Johnny said. "We will focus on removing Ozu from the board. That will be the beginning of our revenge. Perhaps more will follow. Is that what we think?"

"Yes, Johnny. And thanks for getting us to see what we really want," answered Isabella.

261

"I can see that the kind of revenge I want can wait," Gennaro concluded. "There will be time for that. You are both right. Now we need to get our corporation back."

"Ladies and gentlemen of the board, today we decide upon leadership of Rosso International. Malcolm Ozu is contesting my leadership and has asked for a vote on his motion to replace me as chair. Mr. Ozu, you have already spoken about why you think a change is in order and that you should lead that change. Would you like to add anything more?"

"Thank you, Isabella. Board members, realize that this new century calls for new ideas, that the direction of the world economy has shifted to East Asia, and that I, as an East Asian, am in an excellent position to lead this corporation. I trust that you will see the future as I do. I would be honored to have your vote."

Anna Park raised her hand. Ozu was sure he had her on his side. He'd checked with the Sumiyoshi clan. They had paid her a late night visit. "If it pleases the chair,' she began, addressing her words to Isabella, "Could candidate Ozu briefly address the question of women in leadership roles? Thank you."

"Mr. Ozu, your response?" added Isabella.

"Very simply Ms. Park, and it is Ms., not Mrs. or Miss, I assume, I treat women as they treat me, and that goes for everyone. I do not see male or female. I see good or not good business people."

"I understand, Mr. Ozu, but I wonder, do you have any women in key positions in your businesses?"

Ozu was at a momentary loss for words. His face flushed slightly. "Ms. Park, there are so many employees under my guidance that I cannot recall them all."

"Not even one woman?"

"In fact, I am very bad with names and faces."

"But surely you would know whether you have a woman in a management position or any position of importance."

"Let me check my employees with my HR department. I'll get back to you as soon as I possibly can."

"Thank you, Mr.Ozu."

"So, to the business at hand. All those who would like to see Mr. Ozu become chair of Rosso International please raise your hand and say 'Aye.'"

Kim Young Chul raised his hand and said "Aye."

Chi Kai Won followed, "Aye."

Ozu voted for himself. Then a surprise. Guy de Longue raised his hand and said "Aye."

Isabella was shocked. What was going on with de Longue? He'd always been on her side. Now he had voted against her in two recent votes. This gave Ozu four votes, but he needed five. No one else raised a hand.

"Those against. Please raise your hand and say 'Nay.'"

First Anna Park, then Chou Hae. Next Aiello and Gennaro.

"We stand at four to four," Isabella said. "I will vote to break the tie and I vote against."

Ozu glared at Isabella, and then directed his anger to Park and Chou.

"Women cannot rule over men," he said as he left the room.

After the meeting, Isabella cornered de Longue. "Guy, why have you changed sides?"

De Longue looked at her nervously. "I believe in Ozu and East Asia as the future," he said, but he would not make eye contact as he did. He then abruptly walked away.

Johnny met Isabella and Gennaro for a late lunch. "Know what?" Johnny asked. "I checked with my reporter contact. de Longue has been getting pressure from Ozu through the Sumiyoshis. He's frightened. That's why he sided with Ozu. The word is also that Anna Park was threatened by the yakuza.

She was strongly suggested to vote for Ozu. It seems she is made of sterner stuff than de Longue. She didn't cave in. She's staying at the Mandarin Oriental. I think I'll go pay her a visit to thank her."

Johnny knocked on Anna Park's hotel room door. "Hello," he said once, then again in a louder voice. He impulsively gripped the door handle and pushed. The lights were off except for one near the king size bed at the far end of the room. Johnny counted three men and Anna. He could make her out lying supine on her bed, a dark figure hovering over her with a *tanto*, the small sword favored by yakuza. There were two men guarding each side of the entrance to the suite. The first one went for his breast pocket. Johnny didn't have time to think. He grabbed the man's wrist, twisted and turned. Then he made a quick upward movement, breaking the wrist and wrenching the arm from its socket. The yakuza writhed in agony on the hotel room floor. The second man kicked at Johnny's solar plexus. Johnny blocked him with his forearms and delivered a strong blow. He dropped immediately.

Johnny advanced to the figure about to cut Anna with the tanto. "Ozu, don't do it," he yelled. He didn't know whether it was Ozu for sure. He just yelled the first thing that came to him.

"Well, Johnny, my great champion. It seems we meet in combat again. This time for real. Ozu began to circle, holding the tanto in attack position.

When he charged, Johnny sidestepped and tripped him, but as he fell, he swiped at Johnny's rib cage. A bright red spot began to spread.

"One for me, Johnny," Ozu said as he sprang up to attack position again. He went straight at Johnny, but he wasn't fast enough. Johnny grabbed Ozu's wrist and pressed hard on the radial artery. Ozu dropped the sword. Johnny put an arm bar around Ozu's neck and brought him to unconsciousness with a blood choke.

Anna Park lay frozen to her bed. Her eyes were wide and her body was trembling.

"Are you all right, Anna?" asked Johnny.

"I..I think so. He told me was going to make it so no one would look at my face. He would cut my cheeks and lips. I was so frightened, so frightened."

"It's over now. Let's find you another room. I want to leave these three here. Pack your things, Anna, and I will call the front desk." He pulled each man's jacket up over his face, turning the jacket around and buttoning it in back. Then Johnny took the belt from each man's trousers, and wrapped one man's wrists to another's ankles so that all three were hogtied. This done, he called for a new room for Anna, and reported three thieves in her current suite. He suggested that it would be easier for hotel security to handle the problem than to contact the police. Within five minutes, Johnny was escorting Anna into her new room, a simple queen bed and bath next to his own. Johnny didn't care what security did. Ozu and his two yakuza helpers would not try anything more, now that the hotel knew they were there.

CHAPTER TWENTY-FIVE:
Free

Rod Howard was a smart man. He had a PhD in mathematics and his long-time mate, Carl Santoro, was a civil engineer. Rod had worked his way up from party volunteer to party candidate, and now at the age of forty was the new governor of New York State. He was also the first openly gay man to campaign for and to win that position in a New York election. BH, Before Howard, gay mayors, governors, and congressmen often campaigned without identifying themselves as gay. There were few Harvey Milks across the country. Things were different now. Howard was a trail blazer and a poster boy of the new

American moral standard: straight, gay or otherwise, one's sexuality was not per se to be judged.

At the end of his first year, Howard conceived of a plan to allow New York's imprisoned a second chance: each inmate would be completely free the minute he or she left the prison gate. Howard would do this in a New Year's pardon. But he did not do it without digging and researching those who might benefit from such a pardon. His staff interviewed wardens, prison guards, and prisoners to find out which inmates had truly changed and were different people. These were inmates who worked hard, helped others, focused not so much on themselves as on the community that they had involuntarily become part of. Jimmy Diamond was such a person. The police couldn't protest Jimmy's release too loudly. After all, his victim, Sargent Roger Maher, turned out to be a dirty cop, on the take from the Gaeta mob. Jimmy breathed his first breath of freedom five years after imprisonment.

For Jimmy, release from a long prison sentence did not change the person that he was. He was the same person when he went in, and the same person on leaving. He was a good person, who had the interest of others in his heart. But this did not stop Regan Maher from speaking out against the release. Jimmy was front page, lead story news. All New York read about him. That included the children of the Maher family, the family Jimmy had rendered fatherless when he shot and killed Sargent Maher.

When a local New York City reporter stuck a microphone in her face on her way to class at NYU, Regan Maher, grew livid. "He did not deserve a life sentence. He deserved to die. He does not deserve to be released from prison. I guess Governor Howard's got a thing for criminals. Jimmy Diaz is a low life and a murderer. He belongs back in jail."

Up in Woodstock, people were buzzing about Jimmy Diamond. They knew his story. It had spread around town despite the trial being held on the QT. Now he was out of jail and he was big news. People speculated about whether he would leave the area, and reunite with his family. Some said Star wouldn't take him back. Maisie and Davie were old enough to understand it all now. What would they think about their stepfather?

The day Jimmy got released there were tens of reporters with live mics and cameramen supporting them, ready to tape what Jimmy had to say. The story had legs. It would start with reportage and go on to be fodder for op-ed pundits. But Jimmy had nothing to say. He kept his head down after he walked by the last prison guard. He had arranged for Star to pick him up on the road behind the prison. Jimmy had done something clever. Another inmate was being released who was about Jimmy's height and build. That inmate, for a hundred-dollar bill, agreed to walk first, dressed exactly like Jimmy was.

At first, the media swarmed the false Jimmy. This gave the real Jimmy enough time to exit and sprint around the side of the prison to the rear access road. Only a few reporters picked up on it. Jimmy made it to Star's white Ford Escape. He ducked down into the front passenger seat. When Jimmy looked into Star's eyes, he saw love and acceptance. Then, as if snapping out of a reverie, Jimmy asked, "Where's the baby?"

"Davie and Maisie are taking care of him. No worries there, and he loves being with his brother and sister. He's such a good baby. Sleeps through the night. Hardly cries, just for a diaper change or when he's hungry. Smiles at everyone."

"Star, I want to see my son."

"Jimmy, we gotta get out of here right now."

Jimmy hesitated, then realized that Star was looking out for him. "Later then for little Jimmy. Step on it, honey! We're free again. Thank God!"

"We can't stay in town with all those reporters around us...I just don't think so. What do you think?"

"I wish I could give you a good answer. I don't know either. Maybe it's time for us to move, to leave Woodstock. Maybe Canada. No, can't. They wouldn't take a convicted felon like me, would they?"

"I don't know, Jimmy."

"I guess there is a lot we don't know. Maybe the best way to use this time is to start finding out. Just the two of us for a week. What do you say, Star? Somewhere north of here?"

And with that, Star and Jimmy drove upstate to Watervliet, a small town outside of Albany. They checked into a Best Western. And there they spent the next few days catching up on the time they missed as husband and wife. When Star looked into Jimmy's eyes, she saw the same man who loved her and the children, who worked hard to help support the family, who was truly repentant for what he had done in the past.

They disguised themselves. Jimmy cut his hair short, dyed it blond. He put on blue false contacts. Star had done the shopping for it all. She also bought Jimmy a two-piece brown corduroy suit and a black parka at a Goodwill Store in Albany. She dyed her hair a chestnut brown from its original dirty blond color. She bought herself an ankle length beige down coat, warm against the winter chill.

Disguised as best they could, they frequented the libraries in the city of Albany and in the town of Watervliet. They learned that Jimmy would likely be refused entry to Canada. They read as much as they could and surfed the net for places to live. They settled on a small coastal California town named Cambria. Then they returned to the house in Woodstock.

Within a week, they had surreptitiously emptied the house contents into a small U-Haul truck. The crowds of reporters had given up on Jimmy. There were other released felons to interview, after all. The kids were told that they were on a great adventure and they would live where it didn't snow and the ocean was near. They slowly made their way across the country, stopping wherever they thought the kids would enjoy. The baby was as good as gold the whole trip west. Jimmy and Star couldn't believe their luck. He was no problem at all, very portable and happy to be anywhere his family was. They saw the Liberty Bell in Independence National Historical Park in Philadelphia. They visited Lincoln's Log

Cabin outside of Charleston, Illinois. Out west, they visited the Great Salt Lake in Utah, and drove south to the Grand Canyon in Arizona, even gambled a little in Las Vegas. They reached California on a rainy Sunday afternoon. Despite the rain, they walked the Third Street Promenade in Santa Monica after finding a motel on Lincoln Boulevard. They had their first California meal at an In-N-Out Burger.

One stop was left before heading north to Cambria; it was Disneyland.

Monday was sunny. Disneyland was fun. They got there when the gates opened at nine. They left around one o'clock, intent on reaching Cambria before dark. Just before dark, Jimmy, Star, Davie, Maisie, and the baby collapsed on two queen sized beds in the Cambria Shores Motel. They were so tired that the five of them went straight to sleep. The next day would be day one in their new hometown.

Jimmy had let his hair grow back to its natural black color on the trip across country. Star let hers revert to dirty blond. On their first day in town, they looked for a house to rent. They found one in a small town called Cayucos, just twenty minutes south of Cambria on Route One. Davie and Maisie were both enrolled in Coast Union High School. Star found a job in retail at a crafts shop on Burton Drive in Cambria. So, the family spent their days in Cambria. The kids worked part-time after school, so they could commute back to Cayucos with Star. Jimmy bought a used Yamaha V Star 250 and commuted to a gig as a groundskeeper at Hearst Castle in San Simeon. Star found a sitter for little Jimmy the half a day she was at work.

The anonymity the family found in their two years out West in the little towns of Cayucos and Cambria fit them quite well. But over time, each wanted more. Davie was looking at colleges. Maisie wanted her own car. Star needed a better job with benefits and began taking accounting courses at Cuesta College in San Luis Obispo. Jimmy liked working outdoors on the Hearst Castle grounds, but it wasn't enough for him. So, he started to look elsewhere. He and Star began checking out property in and near Cambria. They wanted to build their own home. This new dream animated their days. They spent hours sketching different home designs, discussing the interior layout, looking at furnishings in catalogues. By the fall, Davie had been accepted at the University of Oregon. He was on scholarship, running track. He was thinking about a major in Family and Human Services. He wanted to work with young people who needed help. Maisie had spent more than a year working full time at a local restaurant as a waitress, but that wasn't what she wanted to do with her life. Her eyes were on LA and New York. She wanted to study fashion in one of those cities. Jimmy and Star knew that they wouldn't have Davie and Maisie much longer. They redoubled their efforts to find land and start on their dream house before Maisie left the following year.

Little Jimmy was in love with the Pacific Ocean. The family often walked the boardwalk on Moonstone Beach just over Route One from West Cambria. The baby perked up his ears when he heard crashing waves. He pointed to the beach, his eyes gleaming. It was as if his destiny was unfolding in front of the family. At three years old, little Jimmy, whom they called Junior, was riding a wake board. Within a year, he was on a boogie board. At five years, he had his own surfboard.

Over time it all came together for the Diamond family. They bought a quarter acre lot and set a foundation. The house raised up, all glass and timber with a wrap-around deck on the second floor. The bedrooms were there, too. The first floor was a great room encompassing living room, dining room and kitchen.

Jimmy and Star could hardly believe what they managed to do in five short years. Jimmy was still at Hearst Castle, but he had risen to a foreman's position. Star was now a CPA and made good money working out of the house on her own. Davie had come back for summers when he was at Oregon, but eventually moved to Portland with a girl from his history class. He was working with troubled youth in that city at a YMCA. His girlfriend, Maya, was applying to medical schools. Maisie was in LA at the

Fashion Institute of Design and Merchandising. She did some freelance designing, waited tables, and babysat the children of the spoiled Hollywood rich to make ends meet. But she was on her way. She'd already had offers to work for some of the hottest clothing designers on the West Coast. Within years, the family became an American success story, so far away from what Jimmy Diaz once was.

Meanwhile, Crazy Bobby Gaeta had turned rat on the mob and was naming names and telling tales. It was big news back East, and eventually travelled to the West Coast. Star was the first one to see it.

"Honey, come here for a minute."

"What? Can't it wait. I'm trying to fix the leak in the toilet."

"I think you'd better come here now and see this."

Reluctantly, Jimmy ambled over to the wide screen TV. What he saw caused him to lose a breath. Bobby Gaeta was being led into a courtroom. The crawler under the video read, "Mob boss to tell all."

Jimmy's hair had started to go gray. His mustache was salt and pepper. There were worry lines across his forehead, but none of what he'd been through compared to the awful jolt of fear that ran through his body on seeing Gaeta.

"We've gotta move, Star."

"No, we can't. Everything we built together is here."

"Gaeta will implicate me in other killings. You know I told you what I did for him. If he does, I'm in prison for life. They'll find me easy enough."

"What about the kids?"

"They're not kids anymore. They have their own lives. We have to think about us and about Junior."

"He'll be crushed. He loves his surf spot more than anything, and believe it or not, there's a little blond-haired girl that he shares it with. Her name's Kelly Ann Johnson. She lives with her grandparents just off Moonstone. Her mom and dad were killed in a car accident. She surfs nearly as well as Junior. And they're inseparable in and out of the water. Anyway, where could we go?"

"Canada."

"But I thought we agreed after you got out that we couldn't go to Canada."

"Do you have a better idea?"

"No, it's all too sudden. I need to think."

"There's no time. We have to leave right away."

"Leave it all, all this?"

"Yes. All of it. I'm so goddamn sorry."

Star looked at Jimmy, and made her decision. "Are you sure about Canada?"

"Yeah, the border is long. We can sneak across somewhere."

"I hope so, Jimmy."

The next day they were off. Star's Toyota van was stuffed full of the life they had built in California, including Junior's favorite surfboard. They had a hard time locking up the house. Star cried anew as she walked through every room, remembering what had happened in each one. Jimmy tried to be stoic, but he was eating himself up inside. "The past never rests. It comes back to make my life hell again and again," he thought bitterly. But he hugged Star and held her for a long time as they stood looking at their home, their minds racing through its history, the van engine running.

CHAPTER TWENTY-SIX:
Partners

There were a lot of changes in Isabella Rosso's world since the Ozu episode. She was firmly in charge and the chair of Rosso International. Malcolm Ozu was gone, no longer on the board although he did his best to agitate through the shares he held in stock. The Japanese market was essentially closed to Rosso International. Ozu had gotten that satisfaction. Korea and China were booming as markets, and Ozu's erstwhile allies on the board Kim and Chi, had come around to support Isabella. Profits were too great to do otherwise. De Longue had come to his senses and supported Isabella as well. Finally, Johnny had become a force within the corporation, implementing security programs, hiring personnel, and protecting his sister by doing some of the necessary but tedious work of meeting and greeting people who wanted an audience with her. And so time passed. The corporation flourished.

But neither Isabella nor Johnny could say, "I am happy and fulfilled."

Why was that? Both had given up a large part of their personal lives and private time to the running of the corporation. Romance was never in the air.

Brother and sister lived celibate lives for all the other knew.

Gennaro's wedding in Brooklyn was a very Italian affair. The bride came from a prominent Italian-American family. The food was Italian. The music was Italian. The jokes were Italian, though mostly in English. For once Isabella and Johnny let their hair down. Johnny was pouring them the last of a bottle of Dom Perignon. Isabella smiled at Johnny and primly held out her glass.

"Not too much now," she mock-cautioned him.

"Can I say something?"

"But of course, brother dear."

"Isabella, I never thought I'd see the day that Gennaro married or any of us married for that matter."

"What a strange thing to say! Why?"

"I don't know, just a feeling I've always had. Maybe something to do with us."

"Us?"

"You and me. What we once were. What we became. What we are now."

"And what is that? The now I mean."

"I don't know. I do know that I have a hard time thinking of you as my sister, certainly not my boss…but…"

"Don't you love me…as a sister I mean?"

"No, I don't. Not only that, I mean. I love you as a woman. There, I've said it. Would it be so bad if we were together?"

"Just like that?"

"Yeah, just like that."

"What would people say? Family? The Corporation? Friends? Brother and sister sharing the same bed. Wow! Could never happen."

"It could work if we were careful."

"No, Johnny. Someone'd find out, you know that."

"Then how about tonight? We can slip away. No one would miss us."

And, to Isabella's amazement, they did slip away. In Johnny, Isabella found a warm, loving man who wanted no more than she would give. She was a little out of practice at first, but soon the dam broke, and her emotions flooded her body, and her body responded to her companion's.

In the morning, Isabella nudged Johnny, who was peacefully snoring on his side of the bed. "Wake up, Johnny. You've got to leave."

"Oh, Isabella! Can't we be together just once in the morning light?"

It wasn't hard for her to give in, and neither was it easy to shoo him out of the room afterwards. "Love you, Johnny. Goodbye." Ella had shown Johnny the worst of herself when she was a junkie whore. Now she gave him her best in the strength and passion of her womanhood. Johnny was a lucky man.

Ella and Johnny spent nights together as they could, maintaining privacy as if they were keeping state secrets, and, in a way, they were. Any board member finding out what the two were doing together might claim Johnny was pulling the strings on Isabella or Isabella was too besotted by Johnny to give her all to Rosso International. Fortunately, for Ella and Johnny, they saw each other often enough during business hours that they almost felt like a married couple. But they weren't and could never be if they were to maintain Rosso International.

Legally, first cousins could marry one another and stepbrother and stepsister certainly could. However, in U.S. society, such marriages would not likely be accepted. In 1958, the rocker Jerry Lee Lewis married his thirteen-year old first cousin, Myra Gale Brown. He was subsequently blackballed from radio and went from ten thousand dollars a concert to two hundred fifty dollars a concert. That was over a half century ago and the age gap between Lewis, twenty-two, and his cousin was nine years, but there was no reason to think things had changed enough so that first cousins marrying, especially first cousins in the business world spotlight such as Isabella and Johnny, would be accepted.

Chapter Twenty-Seven:
The North Shore

Ozu Makoto was nothing if not resilient. His time of deepest shame, of fear, of anger was when he lost his seat on the board of Rosso International, when Isabella beat him at his own game of stacking the board.

Then, the Sumiyoshi yakuza family took him back in with the proviso that he earn for them all the capital he lost when he was defeated in his bid for the Rosso International Board. He was protected and could use yakuza muscle to get his way when words weren't enough. But he wasn't free. He was their cash cow, earning not for himself, but for them.

Two years after his separation from Rosso International, he started selling his stock to front men, who would do his bidding but would keep up the air of respectability. These were politicians, bankers, businessmen, and academics. They were to attend shareholder meetings and give the Ozu line, which was essentially to contradict every business venture that Isabella and her board advanced. Most of the time, this did no harm. There were not enough shareholders in opposition because Ozu had had to sell off two- thirds of his holdings in Rosso companies right after he lost the chair of Rosso International just to maintain his lifestyle. He would have sold it all off save for the Sumiyoshi clan controlling him while allowing him to maintain his status as a young business leader in Japanese society, always worthy of front page news. At the same time as he was paying off the Sumiyoshi yakuza, he was squirreling away as much as he could for himself alone. The Sumiyoshi did not know about this. Johnny Rosso did.

Ozu Makoto was determined to get back in the

good graces of the Sumiyoshi clan. "*Oyassan*," Ozu began at a meeting with the head of the clan, "You know that this Rosso female has insulted Japanese honor. She has no respect for this family or for the traditions of our country. I believe it is time we taught her to respect us, better, to serve us. Oyassan, I am nothing. I am young and a nobody. How can I ask your help? It is my giri, my responsibility."

"Eh, Makato-san, you would have me do what exactly? Am I your *wakamono*, your little brother, picking up the shit you drop everywhere?"

"No, Oyassan. Forgive me. I am stupid and clumsy. I only mean to ask your blessing."

"Eh, do what you will. I will not interfere one way or the other. Now go. You have taken up enough of my time."

So Ozu Makoto had let his oyabun know that he would act against Isabella Rosso. He hatched a plan. He knew that Chou Hae and Anna Park had begun a relationship that was beyond business. He further knew that both board members were not 'out'. Each thought it imprudent in her position to do so. He asked to meet with them. They did so one rainy morning in an Asakusa tea room.

"Hello Miss Park and Miss Chou. How are you? I know you must be very curious to know why I've summoned you here, especially because I've been off the board for a few years now. I will put it plainly. I need to speak to Isabella Rosso in private, just her and me alone, but I doubt that she will do so. Therefore, I ask you to create a simple rouse for me. Let her know that you two want to speak to her privately about some women's issues. Make a date to meet in Honolulu. Then, instead of you two, I will be there."

"Why should we help you?" asked Anna.

"Yes, why indeed?" added Chou Hae.

"Because I hold your little secret in my hands like a beautiful butterfly, and if I choose to let it go, it would be most awkward, wouldn't it? Now please allow me to have your cell phones."

Reluctantly, the women acceded to Ozu who then set up a meeting for March fifteenth between the two women and Isabella. It was to be at a house on the North Shore of Oahu, bought with a loan from a Japanese bank that the Sumiyoshi would never repay. Ozu got there two days before to lay his trap with three young *wakamono*, the lowest worker bees in the yakuza hierarchy. Johnny would be traveling with his sister; Ozu's plan was to first draw Johnny away and then deal with Isabella by himself. So, he sent a text message using Anna Park's smart phone. Johnny received the message on landing at Honolulu International. "Meeting site changed. Important you proceed to Kona ASAP. Meet in bar of King Kamehameha Hotel." Johnny told Isabella. She was confused because she had just received a message from Chou Hae telling her the meeting was on at the North Shore house. The siblings decided to split up – Johnny to the Big Island and Isabella on Oahu.

Johnny checked for the next flight to Kona. It wasn't for another two hours, just short enough for him not to chance going to the North Shore and then returning on time for the flight. He bade Isabella goodbye and nervously waited for his flight, texting Anna every five minutes, but getting no response.

Unknown to Ozu, Anna Park and Chou Hae had flown into Oahu the day before because they felt that they were responsible for what might happen between Ozu and Isabella. They were at the North Shore Marriot. The rendezvous house was between the Marriott and Sunset Beach. The two women had rented a car and reconnoitered the house that morning. They saw three young yakuza moving around the property. It looked like they were checking exit routes and access to the adjoining properties. The women thought this a bad sign. Ozu's men were likely ensuring that should Isabella leave the house, they would know where to look for her. As it was, the house was not near the shore, but tucked into the foothills about half mile from it. There was privacy or there was isolation, depending upon who was describing the setting.

Isabella arrived at the house about an hour after deplaning. She was met by one of the wakamonos who spoke some English. "Please to make at home, Missu Loso. Your room secundu fla."

Isabella thought it odd that a young Japanese gangster should act as a greeter for Chou and Park, but tired as she was, she said nothing and went up to her room. After she had had a shower and changed into a black silk top and black capris, she sat on the lanai looking towards the ocean. "No Park and Chou to greet me. A young gangster at the door. What the hell is going on?"

She texted Chou. Then she texted Park. No response. She became apprehensive. She walked downstairs to the front door. There the same young yakuza was stationed as if standing guard. "Pu leez to go in house," he told her as she started to walk outside. Just then a black limo appeared in the drive. Out stepped Malcolm Ozu.

"So good to see you, Isabella. It's been a while, hasn't it?" Ozu smiled his false smile at Isabella. Then he took her elbow to escort her inside. At first she resisted. "Please accompany me inside," he said, his grin getting bigger and his grip on her arm getting stronger.

"You see it's never been about Malcolm and Isabella. It's about Japan and America. About this century and the one past. It is our time now and your time to step down. Feminism is dead. It never really existed in my country. The U.S. is a debtor nation. It is weak and has lost its purpose. The future is Asia, and just as at the end of the nineteenth century, Japan is the natural leader of Asia. I offer you the chance to resign and save face. You retire and name me as your temporary replacement. I will do the rest."

Isabella was totally thrown by the situation, but she soon regained her equilibrium. "Mr. Ozu, you lost fair and square to me. Rosso International has done very well without you. I am in the prime of my working life. Why ever should I resign and give it all to you?"

"If you value your life and your family, you will do as I say. If you don't, you can never move so far away that you are out of my reach. I will kill all of you. Do not doubt it."

Ozu changed tactics. "But this must all come as a shock, and you have had a long flight. Please go to your room and rest. We will call you for dinner and then you must give your answer." And with that, he turned away from Isabella, signaling to a henchman to guide her to her room.

Isabella had to think. She wondered where Anna and Hae were, how they fit into this meeting with Ozu, and who called Johnny away to the Big Island. Her answer would come soon. She tried to assume a meditative asana and let her mind follow her breath, to make it clean and clear, but Ozu's presence intruded into her consciousness and would not go away.

The flight from Tokyo exhausted the old oyabun, but he was determined to settle things with Ozu Makoto. He had done his best to fulfill his promise to bring up Ozu and his sisters. In return, Ozu knew that he must earn for the Sumiyoshi clan, but he kept holding back. He would never learn. That is what the oyabun decided. It was the second time Ozu had taken money from the family by not making all his investments and savings known to them. And it was the second time that they eventually discovered the deceit. This time it was a gaijin, a Rosso brother, who let them know what Ozu was doing. Strange for the oyabun, he told them in fluent Japanese. It was time for judgment, but the oyabun felt partially responsible for Ozu's behavior. After all, Ozu had been brought up in the oyabun's own household.

Johnny never did board the flight to Kona. He had a gut feeling that something was not right, that Isabella faced danger. He was weighing what to do when he received a phone call. It was Anna Park. "Johnny, it's Anna. Ozu is planning something bad for Isabella at a house on the North Shore. Chou Hae and I are here to help you in any way we can. We are sorry, Johnny. We will explain later. Now, go. Just go."

The oyabun and his entourage arrived at the house a half hour before Johnny did. Johnny offered no resistance when one of Ozu's young hoods patted him down and marched him into the house with his hands up.

Now in the downstairs living room each party seemed as surprised as the other to see one another: Ozu for the oyabun, the oyabun for Johnny, Johnny for Ozu. For a few minutes, no one spoke.

The oyabun broke the silence. "What is all this Ozu-chan?"

"It is my time of reckoning with this Western she devil."

"And who is this?" he asked, pointing to Johnny.

"That is her brother. He's nothing. I will take care of both of them."

"And you, Makoto-chan, what have you done? You deceive me a second time."

"How Oyassan? You are my master. I am nothing. What have I done?"

"Hidden money from me." He turned to a

small, bespectacled man in a dark wool suit and tie, incongruous in the warm Hawaiian evening. "You. Bring out the books." The man did as ordered.

"Abe-san takes good care of my money. He noticed that upwards of ten percent of my profits were not coming in. Where could they be? We looked here and there, and then we found your hidden accounts. You are worse than any gaijin. You have no honor, no respect. It is only left for me to decide your end."

"Please, oyassan! I grew up with your children! You are a father to me."

"No, you were once worthy of our family, but now the choice I give you is how to die."

Johnny translated for Isabella, but he could hardly believe what he was hearing. Ozu would die at order of his oyabun. Then he had an idea. "May I make a suggestion?"

"You? Who are you?" the oyabun asked in Japanese.

Johnny responded in that language. This intrigued the oyabun. "You speak our language! Ah, so it was you...Eh! Do you know our customs, too? I wonder. What is your suggestion?"

"That Ozu Makoto die in the ocean."

"How will this happen?"

"He fears water and will panic when he sees the great waves that come to shore here. He will drown."

"Is this true, Makoto-chan? Do you fear the water?"

"I have no fear of water, oyassan."

"Well, then. Let us see."

The strange party of oyabun, yakuza, Ozu, Isabella and Johnny walked the half mile down the foothill road to the shore. There was no moon at all. The sky was black. The waves were crashing, making thunderously loud claps. The oyabun ordered Ozu in the water. Just as he was walking into the near surf, his henchmen pulled out their guns and shot the oyabun and his party dead. That left Isabella and Johnny, who had been trailing the two groups of Japanese.

"Run to the bushes near the road. Get down and stay down, Isabella. I'm going to take care of this."

Johnny walked back along the shoreline. He stripped to his black undershorts to better confuse Ozu's men, who had been ordered to find Isabella and Johnny and kill them. Johnny crept up behind the nearest henchman, his hand over the man's mouth as he put him in a blood choke hold. The henchman fell softly to the sand. Johnny took his gun, put on the man's black shirt and bandana. He silently walked along the shore. Then he saw that the other two were moving towards where Isabella was hiding. He knew he had to be quick. He ran to the first of the two and cold cocked him with the butt of the gun. One left. One who had heard something and was turning toward Johnny.

"What's up?" the wakamono said in Japanese.

"Not here," Johnny answered as the last

henchman approached him.

Before he could pull the trigger, Johnny swept his feet out from under him.

He then pounced on the man and choked him into unconsciousness.

Ozu called out to his men. "Hey, what's going on?"

Johnny ran towards the surf to where Ozu stood. "You're going out to sea, Ozu."

Ozu turned to run, but Johnny was the faster man. He tackled Ozu. He put him in an arm bar and marched him towards the crashing waves.

"We will both die, fool!" cried Ozu.

"Perhaps," Johnny replied. They had gotten far enough in for the surf to unsettle both men, but try as he might, Ozu could not find release even as they were swept underwater, gulping as much water as air. Johnny surfaced and pulled Ozu up. "We'll wait for a big one. It'll be your last ride."

And it came. Johnny ducked underwater. Ozu got the full brunt of a fifteen-foot wave. It took all Johnny had to claw his way back to shore, the undertow wanting to push him out to sea. He waited for a minute, panting to get his breath back, looking at the thunderous waves pounding the shore. Could he see Ozu? As he was turning back to find Isabella, he glanced over his shoulder and vaguely imagined a hand waving wildly.

Ozu was never seen again, nor were his three henchmen. Johnny imagined they'd got the first plane back to Tokyo when they could not find Ozu, but found the bodies of the oyabun and his men instead, a reminder that they could be arrested by the Hawaiian police if they stayed around.

After a phone call, Johnny and Isabella met up with Anna Park and Chou Hae at their hotel. The women apologized and offered their resignations. Isabella wouldn't hear of it.

CHAPTER TWENTY-EIGHT:
Cape Verde

Canada was a good first move. They didn't have to sneak across the border after all; because of Jimmy's pardon, Canada accepted him. But soon after, Crazy Bobby Gaeta's testimony about Jimmy's wet work was on the CBC nationwide. Gaeta named Jimmy in five hits, all mob-related; the U.S. would probably move for extradition. He and Star had a decision to make. They had to go somewhere that had no extradition treaty with the United States. Jimmy vowed he would never return in handcuffs. The couple also needed to think about their young son and what was good for him. Their first thought was

Cuba. It was warm and close to the U.S. But after talking it through, they decided on another destination.

"Jimmy, Cuba's warm and it's opening up to the U.S. now."

"Yeah, I thought about it, but…"

"But what?"

"It's too close and too indefinite. You don't know what'll happen next there after the second Castro goes and the U.S. digs into the economy again. They could easily agree on an extradition treaty down the road."

"Then where?"

"How's your Portuguese?"

"Funny man! How's yours?"

"Non-existent, but I can learn. After all, it's a little like Spanish."

"So where to?"

"I've done some research. Cape Verde. They're islands in the Atlantic Ocean. The government's good and there're lots of Portuguese there. It's a mixed society with a European vibe."

"I don't know anything about it. I've never even heard of it."

"So much the better. It's off the radar. To get there, you gotta really make an effort. We could settle there. I feel it. It's right for us. We'll go to Praia, the capital on the island of Santiago. It's over a hundred thousand people, and the cost of living is cheap."

Star smiled. "Okay, Jimmy Diamond. I can see that you've done your homework, so let's go! God! I hope it's our last time moving."

"It will be Star. It will be. I promise. And it'll be good for Junior. Great surfing they say."

Vancouver to Mexico, and then to Portugal. Visa for Cape Verde in Lisbon. Fly to Cape Verde. This was the tricky part, getting the visa and getting to the island legally. Luckily for Jimmy and Star, there was no U.S. APB for Jimmy. He didn't make the INTERPOL wanted list. The U.S. authorities had apparently decided not to pursue Jimmy. Thus, there was no new official information related to him which would cause a government agent to pull him out of an entry line into a little room for questioning.

Jimmy and Star found a little house to rent just outside of Praia. With time, both learned passable Portuguese, and as they were live-and-let-live kind of people, they were accepted by their Cape Verdean neighbors. Their acceptance was accelerated because of the universal ice breaker, a child. The Verdeans took to Junior right away. He went to school, learned Portuguese, had lots of friends and surfed every day.

The family went through legal procedures and eventually became permanent residents. After a few years of scraping together a living – Star giving English lessons and Jimmy fishing -they bought a house big enough to accommodate themselves and to become a bed and breakfast named "3,000 Miles From Woodstock." The name had great appeal to aging hippies and fans of the sixties. Jimmy and Star got a yearly Christmas visit from Davie and his family, who lived in Seattle, where Davie ran a youth program for the city. He was married with three kids and a pediatrician for a wife. Maisie was part of the international fashion world, and was often on a plane to Europe. This made her visits more frequent, but less predictable. She was the one who thought of the name, and brought lots of sixties photos to hang in the rooms: Carnaby Street, Flower Power, Beatles, Stones, The Dead, Woodstock, hippies, Janis, Jimi, Altamont.

Perhaps the biggest surprise was Kelly Ann Johnson's arrival. She and Junior had been corresponding on social media, and they were determined to be reunited. Junior, who now went by Jaco, was ecstatic.

Kelly Ann came that second summer with her guardian, a woman surfer named Windy McCall. Windy was, to Kelly Ann, a big sister and mother combined. The three surfers had a great time that first summer together. The best surf spots were theirs.

Cape Verde has great surfing, but when Jaco and Kelly Ann were together that first time, there were only a few adventurous outsiders, and a few locals surfing. Most islanders thought the surf too dangerous. Die-hard surfers who came later loved the challenge.

Jaco and Kelly Ann's story was something out of a fairy tale. They became closer and closer to each other as surfing partners and life partners. At just eighteen, Jaco, and nineteen, Kelly Ann, they married and set up house on the island. Two happier people would have been hard to find anywhere.

Jimmy's past was behind him. No one wanted to put him in jail anymore, save Regan Maher, and even she gave up her quest although she was always good for a sound bite when a cop with a family was killed in New York City. Crazy Bobby Gaeta was behind bars. The rumor mill had it that there was a contract on him inside.

One evening, just before sunset, Jimmy was

312

sitting on a boulder, looking out into the endless Atlantic. Star had just finished preparing dinner for their several guests, and had a few minutes to catch her breath.

"Whatcha thinking Jimmy?"

"How lucky I am to be here with you. How beautiful life can be. I am happy."

"I love you Jimmy Diamond," she said as she rose and kissed him on the forehead. "But it's back to the kitchen for both of us."

"Sure, honey. Just one last look at the ocean. You never know when you'll have another."

"Oh, stop it! We've got every day for the rest of our lives to listen to the waves and watch the sunset over the ocean."

"Everyday. Everyday," repeated Jimmy.

CHAPTER TWENTY-NINE:
The Business of Life

Change was in the air for Isabella and Johnny. The first step was taken by Isabella at a Rosso International Board meeting one lazy August afternoon.

"And so, I offer my resignation, non-negotiable. I am retiring from Rosso International, a company in which I followed my mother and that you have fostered and nurtured over time. I will, of course, retain my shares in the company, and Gennaro will continue on the board. You might consider adding another Rosso sibling, Gildo, but that is entirely up to you. I am not sure of my next step, but I am sure that

315

it is time to go. Thanks to all of you for your loyalty and your support."

The shock wave moved through the board room, creating a deep silence. Finally, Anna Park spoke. "Thank you, Isabella, for your leadership, for putting people before profit, for allowing us to grow into our responsibilities over time. I will miss you. We all will." And with that each board member stood and applauded. Isabella smiled at each of them, and each smiled in return.

In the weeks that followed, Isabella went on a retreat in the mountains of central California. She bathed herself in the natural silence of the New Camaldoli Hermitage. She walked and she thought. She began a daily program of yoga and meditation. She felt her body and mind come together in a way that began to heal the scars of her life. She thought about Johnny. She thought about him a lot. In the end, she decided that they were right for each other as partners, but she thought their kinship created problems for a sexual relationship.

When she came down from the hermitage, Johnny was already at the Ragged Point Inn, patiently waiting for Isabella to join him. He opened his arms to embrace her.

"For the last time as lovers," she said to him as he pulled her into the room. "Johnny, we will always be together, but I'm not sure I can continue our relationship in the way you would like. You know what I mean."

"I kind of guessed that might be the case when you told me you were going to a hermitage full of celibate monks. So what is next for us? You know I will love you any way you want me to."

That night they made love, not wanting it to end, but knowing it must. In the morning, they lay still, wrapped in each other's arms.

Johnny spoke first. "You know I resigned, too, just this week while you were up in the mountains."

"I thought you would, no I hoped with all my heart that you would, so you could be with me."

317

"So, Ella, what's next for us?"

"Brooklyn."

"Brooklyn?"

"Yes, remember the junkie who could barely move without her pimp telling her to? Well, there are others like her and they need the help we can provide -- a wellness center."

"A what?"

"A center where whores, pimps, street kids, gang bangers, the whole cast of suffering humanity in the city, a place where they can heal."

Johnny's eyes opened wide. "Full circle! We're going full circle, but in a good way. I like it. I really like it."

"The Rosso Center for Healing. How about that for a name?"

"Sounds good to me. But, tell me about us. Do you think we can never be together in this way again?"

"Who knows the future, Johnny? *Che sara' sara'.*"

That night Johnny dreamed of the redhead again. She was standing facing him with a smile as big as the sun, a smile so bright that Johnny couldn't hold her gaze. He had to look away. When he looked up again, the redhead had become Ella. "Love you, Johnny," she said. Johnny smiled.

"What was so wonderful? You had this huge grin on your face," Ella asked him as she gently shook him awake.

"Mmm. Good dream. Say Ella, is your hair getting redder or is it just the way the sunlight is hitting it from the window?"

"A bit redder. I found more gray hairs than I wanted on my brush, so I brought a hair dye with me to the hermitage. It's strawberry blonde. Do you like it?"

"Very much."

Author's Biography

Lou Spaventa was born in Brooklyn, New York, but a desire to see and know something beyond city borders set him on a path to East Asia, Europe, the Middle East, the Caribbean and South America, and began a lifelong interest in language and culture.

He became a Peace Corps Volunteer, a teacher trainer, a Fulbright lecturer, a U.S. foreign service officer., and finally a professor of English Skills at Santa Barbara City College. Lou has written and co-written several books and has been an online columnist.

He is an avid swimmer and a semi-professional musician. He lives in Santa Barbara, California.

To contact the author Lou Spaventa, or to find out more about other works of the author, please visit the website:

http://www.ALifeInWords.com

56192041R00202

Made in the USA
San Bernardino, CA
09 November 2017